LOOKING FOR LOVE

Fleur's sweetheart, Tom, disappeared after being conscripted into the Army during the Vietnam War. Twenty years later, Fleur finds a package of his unread letters, intercepted and hidden by her widowed mother. From them, she learns that he felt betrayed by her silence. Dismayed, but determined to explain, Fleur engages Lucas, a private investigator, to help in the search that takes them to Vietnam. Will she find Tom there and put right the wrong?

ZELMA FALKINER

LOOKING FOR LOVE

Complete and Unabridged

LINFORD
Leicester

First published in Great Britain in 2006

First Linford Edition
published 2007

British Library CIP Data

Falkiner, Zelma
    Looking for love.—Large print ed.—
Linford romance library
1. Vietnam War, *1961 – 1975* —Missing
in action—Fiction 2. Love stories
3. Large type books
I. Title
823.9'2 [F]

ISBN 978–1–84617–755–2

Published by
F. A. Thorpe (Publishing)
Anstey, Leicestershire

Set by Words & Graphics Ltd.
Anstey, Leicestershire
Printed and bound in Great Britain by
T. J. International Ltd., Padstow, Cornwall

This book is printed on acid-free paper

1

AUSTRALIA, 1988

Umbrellas sprouted like mushrooms on the lawn in front of the house as soft rain crept across the garden from the west. It had held off long enough for a good crowd to gather for the auction, and for spirited bidding to push the price past the reserve.

'Ladies and gentlemen, this is your last chance to buy a beautiful older-style home, in a sought-after suburb. My instructions are that the property is to be sold. Are you all done?'

Fleur Mitchell watched from her vantage point by the big bay window in the front room as, one more time, the auctioneer's eagle-eye raked the crowd.

'Last call, going . . . going . . . ' The raised arm fell, the contract papers slapped against his palm. 'Gone!'

The finality of the sale brought a surprising rush of relief, not sadness, to Fleur. It was over. She had done her duty. She was free!

'Sold to the couple standing under the tree. Congratulations, you've bought a sound piece of property,' the auctioneer went on. 'Will you come this way, please.'

Fleur turned from the window to greet the couple as they entered the room.

'An excellent result,' remarked the auctioneer's assistant in an aside to her, before making the introductions.

'I hope you'll be as happy here as my mother and I were,' she murmured as she shook hands with the new owners. She wasn't sure that was exactly the truth. No-one's life is all happy times, but it seemed the thing to say.

'Paid a little more than we expected, but Sharon here had her heart set on it, and I like to give her what she wants,' the husband boasted. 'Good thing for you, eh?'

'I expect you'll be sorry to leave this

lovely home,' the young wife said sympathetically.

Fleur nodded, as was expected of her, but it definitely wasn't true. This part of her life was over, already behind her. There would be formalities to complete, settlement day to be arranged but the end was in sight.

'With me teaching full-time, the house and garden were getting too much for my mother,' she said. It was another suitable explanation to give to strangers. 'She is happily settled in a retirement village, enjoying the amenities without the responsibilities of a house.'

That was the part Fleur liked the best. The daily care of her mother was no longer her responsibility. The chosen facility catered for a client's every wish. And her mother always had plenty of those, even before arthritis made life difficult for her. As an only child, and a daughter, Fleur had had more than her fair share of demands made on her.

After a chance visit to a resident, it

had become Elaine Mitchell's wish to go into the War Widows Assisted Living Accommodation. And make it seem as if all her motives were unselfish.

'Life is passing you by while you're looking after me. The older you get the more bitter and twisted you will become,' she had explained when she brought up the subject, months before.

'Are you saying I'm bitter and twisted?' Fleur had asked with a laugh, knowing it wasn't true.

'No, I'm not saying that. You have always had a pleasant disposition. And you've been a dutiful daughter.'

Fleur had smiled at her mother's reluctance to say anything that might, as she would put it, give her daughter a swelled head. 'That's faint praise, Mother.'

'Although you're slow to trust people, especially when it comes to men,' her mother went on, scarcely pausing for breath. 'It's not very Christian-like.'

Fleur hoped her mother wasn't going

to get on her religious hobby-horse. They'd been over that ground before.

'You don't allow yourself the luxury of trusting men when you've been dumped by one,' Fleur retorted, still without rancour. They'd been over this, too. Over and over, for the past twenty years.

'I wish you wouldn't use that word,' Elaine Mitchell protested.

'Dumped, deserted, call it what you will, the result has been the same. The fact is, Tom went away to the war and didn't bother to write.'

'But it isn't very nice to talk like that . . .'

Fleur waved her hands, dismissing it as unimportant. 'It's all right. It was a long time ago. It hurt then, but I'm a big girl now and big girls get on with life. And talking of getting on, why don't we sort this room before dinner?'

'Not now, Fleur,' her mother had answered, a steely note creeping into her voice.

Fleur sighed. Her mother could be

stubborn sometimes. She wondered if it was worth insisting and decided it wasn't. Although the decision to sell up and move had been made, it would probably be weeks before a buyer could be found and there was the need for action about their belongings.

It hadn't turned out that way. The real estate agents had proved very efficient, anxious to schedule an auction before summer was over. They had quickly found a new home for her, vacant possession.

Moving her mother and her chosen pieces of furniture into the retirement village had become a rush job, right in the middle of end-of-term assessments at school. It had been exhausting, the last thing she needed.

'Miss Mitchell?'

The auctioneer's voice broke into her reverie. With the new owners' signatures on the contract, he and his staff were anxious to move on to the next sale.

Fleur watched from the veranda as

they scurried through the thickening rain to their car, removing the directional signs as they went.

Shivering in the damp air, she stepped back inside and closed the door. The house seemed forlorn, too. Stripped of their personal belongings, the almost empty rooms no longer bore a resemblance to the home Fleur had lived in all her life.

Fleur decided what she needed was a good, strong cup of tea, and strode purposefully down the passage toward the kitchen. Cold and clinical in its emptiness, without even the comforting hum of the refrigerator, it wasn't a place to linger in.

Carrying the tea-tray, she went back down the hallway to the sitting-room.

Taking up one main wall was the small roll-top desk, another piece of furniture that neither she or her mother wanted in their new home.

Repeated earlier refusals by Elaine Mitchell to attend to its clearance had ended as Fleur expected, with her left to sift through the papers.

She glanced at her watch. Although the day was darkening still further, there was enough time left before she returned to her new home for the night. She gathered up two cardboard boxes and, with a sigh, knelt before the desk, pulled out the first of its lower drawers and began sorting.

Once both sets of drawers were cleared, Fleur stood up and turned the key in the roll-top. It slid back to reveal under-utilised shelves and pigeon-holes. Systematically, she emptied each compartment until only one small drawer remained. It was locked.

She fingered through the bunch of keys, which, until now, had been jealously guarded by her mother. She hadn't thought that unusual. Growing up she accepted that her mother had secrets, all adults did, and was incurious. Even when she was older and the financial arrangements of their life became another of her duties, she indulged her mother.

At last, one of the keys fitted the lock. As she turned it she smiled, wondering what she might discover. Probably some discarded and long-forgotten momento of the past.

A wad of letters, held together by a rubber-band, filled the drawer. Her smile deepened. Her mother's love-letters! As Fleur lifted them out her own name leapt at her from the top envelope. She felt the stirring of foreboding.

Carefully, with fingers stiffened by apprehension, Fleur turned back the first letter, to reveal her name and address on the second. And the third. Under pressure, the perished rubber-band snapped and the parcel of letters burst free of her hands and scattered at her feet. Uncomprehending, she stared down at them.

Those that landed face-up all bore her name and address, but amongst them were others that fell face-down. These carried an Australian army camp return-to-sender address on the flip-side. All written in a familiar hand. Tom's!

Quite mechanically she bent and, with shaking hands, gathered them up. Her mind struggled to understand, torn by conflicting messages. Tom had written! He had not walked away from her!

After twenty years of thinking otherwise it was hard to believe. But what were his letters doing locked in a compartment in her mother's desk? What did it mean?

There could by only one explanation. Elaine Mitchell had intercepted them.

Fleur found it impossible to accept the idea, it was too far-fetched. The strength drained from her legs. Blindly, she grabbed the back of the armchair for support and felt her way around it to sink into its depths. Why would her mother do such a thing? Certainly not to read what Tom had written; the letters were all unopened.

And unread. The enormity of their loss unleashed a parade of emotions in

Fleur. The remembered pain of the long years shuddered through her, together with regret for her now wrongful accusations of Tom's broken promises.

Although it was too late, a lifetime too late, she desperately needed to know what he had said to her, all those years ago. She fumbled through the box beside her until she found the letter-opener, used it and methodically arranged the letters in sequence. Leaning back in the chair, she began reading.

★ ★ ★

The first began with Tom's pet name for her, *My darling flower-child*. She recognised the play of words on her name and the hippy times. And even though he was only two years older than her, he joked often about their age difference, claiming that made him wiser.

His age was no longer a joke when conscription for the Vietnam war became law. This meant he was eligible for the national ballot of twenty-year olds. It had all the luck of a lottery, and when he received his call-up papers, Fleur hadn't wanted him to go. She had plans for them to marry and settle down to raise a family.

Tearfully, she had farewelled him, full of hope that it wouldn't be for long. How wrong she'd been.

The first letter was full of the tedious train journey to the tropical north of Australia, to the jungle training camp at Canungra. As the army took over his life, homesickness surfaced in the next letters, and longings for some word from her.

Fleur almost broke down when she reached this point. Even after the intervening years, the thought of Tom, lonely, needing reassurance and not getting it, tore at her heart.

The return address on the envelopes had changed to an army post office to become unidentifiable and, although he didn't say so, Fleur knew that meant he was in a battle zone. Bewilderment and doubts had crept into the letters.

I wouldn't have thought it too difficult for you, in the comfort of your home, to spare me the time to let me know you're all right and that you still love me, he wrote. *It is hell enough without this.*

Fleur shifted restlessly in her chair. The warmth of the fire was no match for the bleakness that enveloped her.

She expected that from here on the letters would become even sadder because she hadn't answered, but she wasn't prepared for the bitterness, the pointed accusations, the insulting questions. It was if the war had changed him.

Is it a case of out of sight, out of mind? he asked in one. *You could at least send me a Dear John letter, or don't you have the decency to do that? Some fellows here are getting them already, so you wouldn't be starting a new trend.*

In another, the poignancy of his question, *Do you take me for a fool?* brought tears to Fleur's eyes, so that she could no longer see. Impatiently, she fumbled in a pocket for a handkerchief, wiped them away and opened the last letter.

In it, Tom had finally put their future into plain English. *I plead guilty to loving you from the first time I saw you in the school staff-room. That was a mistake, one I'll never make again, not with any woman. I get the message, Fleur. It is over. I won't bother you any more.*

Scalding tears became twin streams down her face.

* * *

All week, Fleur made excuses to stay away from visiting the War Widows' village, afraid to face her mother whilst her anger was so high. She wondered if it would ever subside.

Twenty years of wasted lives! What

Elaine Mitchell had done was monstrous and yet one part of Fleur wanted there to be a good reason. This was her mother, after all.

Going through her days on automatic, she knew she needed to get it into perspective before any confrontation, and to choose the right moment. There was always the threat of triggering an emotional storm in her mother that could bring on a heart attack. But would there ever be a right moment for what she had to say to her.

When it couldn't be postponed any longer, Fleur drove to the retirement village. Elaine Mitchell was waiting in a wheelchair at the edge of the carpark.

Fleur was dismayed.

'Why are you in the wheelchair? I thought your mobility was improving in the specially-designed unit. Wouldn't the doctor want you to use the walking-frame as much as possible?'

'I had someone bring me down here. I thought you could take me through the gardens back to my unit,' explained her mother. 'That would be too far for me to walk.'

Still fixed on the discovery of Tom's letters, Fleur quashed the instant thought that this was a delaying tactic. Her mother couldn't know they had been found. Damping down her suspicions, she pushed the wheelchair along the paths of the extensive gardens.

'I'll make us tea,' she said as soon as they were in the unit, expecting her mother to give up the wheelchair once they were inside. She didn't. It was a bad sign.

'Shouldn't you be getting out of the wheelchair, Mother?'

'Don't fuss,' Elaine Mitchell replied, manoeuvring herself into position at the window that looked out over the village.

'But — '

'Don't fuss!'

Fleur realised it wasn't going to be easy challenging her mother about the letters, but she desperately needed answers. Without them she was in danger of becoming bitter and twisted, as her mother had suggested she would, but not because of the responsibility of an invalid.

She had to ask. 'Mother, I found a package of Tom's letters in the desk . . . '

The figure in the wheelchair started and became ramrod-stiff. Fleur decided she had been right and that her mother had forgotten all about them.

'You kept them from me?' Fleur asked, hoping for the impossible, for some acceptable explanation.

'Yes,' replied her mother, still not turning the chair to face her.

Fleur struggled to control the warring emotions that rose in her and threatened to overcome her best intentions. Love and pity for the woman who had reared her on her own was being swamped by angry despair.

'But why?' she cried.

'I didn't want you to be a war widow like me and subjected to a lonely life.' There was defiance in every line of the frail body.

Fleur realised her mother couldn't see the irony of it. She might as well be widowed. Tom had been lost to her as surely as if he had died.

'I suppose you did it out of love for me,' she said in a voice devoid of any criticism.

The woman in the wheelchair turned at that, eagerly taking up the excuse.

'Yes, yes, a mother knows best about these things. I wanted to spare you.'

And I'm expected to spare you, Fleur thought, because you're my invalid mother and only did what you thought was best.

Unfortunately, it wasn't the best, not for me. Or for Tom. The best would have been each of us knowing the other cared, whatever the outcome of his war service. Time hadn't wiped out that need.

2

The noise in the staff room had reached a Friday afternoon fever pitch. Everyone had something to say, talking over each other as they made arrangements for the weekend and prepared to leave.

At last, there was an exodus of the younger staff members. In the quiet that followed, Fleur began tidying the room.

'Phew! Oh, what it is to be young!' exclaimed thirty-year-old Camille, helping herself to a fresh cup of coffee.

'And noisy!' agreed Fieur. She offered the headmaster the last of the afternoon-tea cakes.

'Listen to you two old things,' he scoffed benignly, taking the only scone left on the plate. 'Who was it said youth is wasted on the young? You both have a lot of good years ahead of you, and in my school, I hope.'

The talk of the years ahead only reminded Fleur of the years that had been wasted. All week she'd wrestled with the discovery of the letters and how best to cope with that knowledge. Sink into self-pity or do something positive?

Phillip Bennett was looking closely at her. 'Surely you're not worried about your age? There's not a grey hair in sight, not like me.' He put up a hand and patted his head of salt-and-pepper hair.

'Well, I'm not worried really, not about that,' she said. He raised a quizzical eyebrow. 'But there is something on my mind, I must admit. A bizarre thing has happened. Do you remember Tom Drysdale?'

'Why, yes, I do. Had the makings of a good teacher. Called up for the Vietnam War, wasn't he? What happened to him? Not killed in action, I hope.'

Fleur thrust that possibility from her mind. It was something too awful to contemplate. She toyed with her teaspoon. How much should she tell

Phillip Bennett? Everything, she decided, everything but her mother's role in the story. There was nothing to be gained by doing that.

'I don't know what happened to him,' she confessed. 'But I want to find out. You see, there was a misunderstanding and he disappeared from my life twenty years ago.'

'Do I sense there was a secret romance? Unrequited love, perhaps? I can't wait to tell my wife. She will enjoy this. She always sees everything in romantic terms, and I have to say, she is seldom wrong in these matters.'

Fleur could see it was useless to even think of half-telling the story. The Bennetts had known her too long, twenty years, in fact.

'Yes, there was a romance between us, nothing official, unfortunately, as it now turns out. His letters to me from the war zone were . . . er, mislaid. I never got them.'

'What do you mean, mislaid?' Camille, her face alive with interest, wanted more details. 'By the post office?'

'No, but let's just leave it at that. What has happened is they have turned up. And . . . I have to find him to tell him that.'

'Have you tried through official channels?' asked Phillip Bennett.

'Yes, but because we weren't even engaged, the Army won't give out information.'

'There must be something we can do.' The headmaster furrowed his brow in concentration. 'I seem to remember hearing about a group of Vietnam veterans living on a farm somewhere out in the bush beyond Red Hill. They keep pretty well to themselves, I believe, no-one ever sees them. They might be able to give you some information that would help in the search. Perhaps I could make enquiries on your behalf.'

Fleur was hesitant to impose, but agreed it could prove helpful, a starting point. 'If you're sure it won't be any trouble . . . '

But Camille's quick mind had already come up with a more immediate solution.

'Get yourself a private investigator,' she advised.

* * *

The address given in the advertisement for the private investigator's office was as Fleur would have expected. A narrow street, little more than an alleyway, hemmed in by old, dark buildings, was enough to make her hesitate before leaving the comfort of the busy street behind her.

Suddenly, she wished she hadn't allowed Camille to persuade her to take this course of action. Good sense told her she should let the headmaster make enquiries for her. The veterans could tell her where and how to look for Tom. In time.

She took a deep breath and plunged into the street, checking the haphazard numbering against her notebook as she went. It was strangely quiet, apart from the sound of her clicking heels echoing off the walls.

Her search didn't take long. An understated sign affixed over a security intercom gave no indication of the profession of the man she was seeking.

Fleur answered the disembodied female voice with her name as requested and was rewarded with the release of the safety catch. Inside, the stairwell was full of light, the stairs covered with good-quality carpet.

At the top of the first flight, a glass door opened into a reception area. It was surprisingly business-like, not at all as she had expected. In fact, she could easily have been on a visit to a financial advisor, or a medical specialist.

The owner of the voice, a pleasant-looking girl, removed the dictation ear-plugs and stood up. A name plate on the desk gave her name as Karen.

'Miss Mitchell. Come with me,' she invited, leading the way. 'Lucas is waiting for you.'

The use of her boss's first name was the only less-than-formal note.

Karen knocked on an inner door, opened it and announced the new client. The last of Fleur's pre-conceived ideas of what a private investigator's office would or should be like, disappeared.

The pale grey walls and darker carpet continued in Lucas Gray's light-filled office. Was this a deliberate play on his name? The thought was chased from her mind as he rose from behind the orderly desk.

This was no slovenly, worldly-wise man with nicotine-stained fingers reaching into the bottom drawer for a bottle.

Lucas Gray was about her age and wore a dark suit, fresh white shirt and tasteful tie. He looked like any businessman to be seen going about the streets of the city. Except for the eyes that looked back at her from under a stray forelock of dark hair — they were blue, but a piercing blue. Nothing much would get past them, she decided.

'You look surprised,' he said, coming forward to greet her. 'What or whom were you expecting?'

'I haven't been keeping up with the advances in private investigation,' she said, slightly embarrassed that her naivety was showing. 'I'm stuck back with the late-night black and white movies and Humphrey Bogart.'

The private investigator smiled and pulled out the chair for Fleur to sit. Back behind his desk, he locked his fingers into a fist under his chin and leaned forward on his elbows.

'And what can I do for you, Miss Mitchell?'

Fleur wondered if all his clients felt overwhelmed by the unexpectedness of the man. Dismay followed. Would the all-seeing, all-knowing eyes pick up on that?

'I want to find a soldier who went away to the Vietnam War . . . ' Her words trailed off as she realised this man was the first person she'd had to actually face with her request for help. It had been easier making enquiries over the phone. What if he laughed at her? Twenty years was a long time, and she knew so little.

Lucas Gray didn't laugh. He took up his pen and held it poised over the form on the desk in front of him.

'His name, rank, unit, last known address?'

Unable to trust her voice, Fleur pushed the first of Tom's letters across the desk for him to copy the details.

'Your relationship to — ' he studied the back of the envelope. 'To Private Drysdale?'

'That seems to be the trouble. I've been in touch with Army Records but because I have no official status . . . ' Her voice trailed off again. That had been her first disappointment, when the Army refused to supply her with any information at all.

The private investigator nodded. 'Did you try the Vietnam Veterans' Association?'

That had been another disappointment. 'They were sympathetic, but told me about three percent of the veterans weren't registered or didn't want their name and whereabouts divulged. That was when I decided to come to you.'

He nodded again. 'It was a very unpopular war. There was so much ill-feeling in the community when they came back, no welcoming parades, no recognition. Some of them are still very bitter.'

Fleur knew Tom had become bitter, but not about the war. She wondered should she tell Lucas Gray that?

'I should warn you it might be difficult to find Private Drysdale if he doesn't want to be found,' he went on.

'I understand what you are saying, Mr Gray — '

'Lucas, please. Because of the often personal nature of our assignments, we don't stand on ceremony here. This is obviously one of those occasions.'

With an abrupt movement that startled her, the private investigator rose from his chair, crossed the room and began searching in a filing cabinet.

'It is going to make my enquiries easier if I am able to emphasise it is personal rather than recriminatory. As I said, the Vietnam veterans are still very close-knit and loyal to each other.'

Fleur had to swivel in her chair to catch his conversation.

'I will need to know where he was born, who were his next-of-kin — '

'I don't have that information. He was a teacher at our school.'

'Good! The Education Department! There's a starting point.'

Fleur suddenly felt very silly. She knew so little about Tom's background. It hadn't seemed very important then. They were all flower children and, as the song went, 'the times were a changin''.

Her mother hadn't approved of those changes. She disliked the long, flowing dresses that were being worn, the beads and the free and easy ways of young people.

Fleur couldn't shake off the conviction that this was the real reason Elaine Mitchell had intercepted his letters.

There hadn't been any need to do that — the war would have changed Tom. It changed the whole country.

Lucas Gray had found the reference he needed and returned to his chair. He was so business-like her request suddenly seemed frivolous to Fleur. She should never have come.

'I'm sorry, I think I've wasted your time. However will you find him with so little to go on? Where will you begin? It's impossible,' she said, preparing to leave.

He waved aside her protestations. 'You'd be surprised how easy it is. Most people leave a trail. I'll check the electoral roll to begin with, credit rating, police records, that sort of thing.'

The piercing blue eyes took in his client's worried face. He leaned forward. 'Trust me, I'll find Tom Drysdale for you,' he promised.

Settled in her new home, finding Tom became Fleur's main preoccupation. Although it wasn't quite two weeks since her visit to Lucas Gray, she fretted at not having received a report from him. Surely checking the records wouldn't take so long.

Just as she was on the verge of ringing the private investigator, Phillip Bennet called her into his office during one of her pupil-free periods.

'Here is the name of the farm where the Vietnam veterans live,' he said, handing her a slip of paper. 'It's a curriculum day tomorrow. I think we could excuse you if you'd like to follow it up.'

The farm was in a picturesque part of the country, given over to cattle grazing. The isolated homestead stood well back from the road, almost obscured by a thick belt of trees.

It wasn't until Fleur was up close that she saw the trees also obscured a

31

six-foot chain-mesh fence topped with razor-wire. The drive ended at a padlocked gate.

She cut the engine and got out, surprised to find the way so effectively barred. As she neared the gate two ferocious-looking Doberman guard-dogs leapt out of kennels inside the fence and set up barking.

She shrank back instinctively, not quite trusting the gate was strong enough to withstand the dogs' combined weight as they flung themselves against it, fangs bared and dripping saliva.

'Stand right there, lady,' ordered a voice behind her.

Fleur jumped and swung around. Outlined against the setting sun was a man in army fatigues, carrying an army-type gun. It pointed in her direction.

Her heart pounded against her rib cage. Whatever was happening? Where had he come from? She hadn't heard his steps on the gravel. Was this an army establishment?

'What are you doing here?' the man asked, his voice matching the menace of his gun.

'I . . . I . . . ' It was no good, her mouth was too dry to form words. Her eyes measured the distance between herself and the car and dismissed the idea of making a run for it. He looked as if he might use his weapon.

The appearance of the man hadn't quietened the dogs on the other side of the fence. They kept up their frenzied barking.

Fleur tried again. 'I . . . I came to ask . . . for your help,' she said.

'This is not the place to ask for help,' he said, advancing on her. 'Tell the truth. Why are you here?'

'I'm looking for help to find someone who went away to the Vietnam War . . . and no-one will give me any information.'

The face under the well-worn army hat darkened. 'Information? You wouldn't be a reporter by any chance, would you? You have the look of one,' he sneered.

'A reporter? No, I'm a school teacher.'

He moved closer. Fleur backed away until she felt the side of the car behind her. She could go no farther. Fear engulfed her, draining the strength from her body.

The man kept coming, his gun still held at the ready. Its barrel dug into her stomach, the metal cold and unyielding through her light dress.

'Listen, lady, get out of here while you still can.'

3

Back on the main road, her hands still trembling from the threat, her mind asking why, Fleur paid little attention to what seemed to be a small van behind her, its lights set on low beam.

For some time it stayed there, its presence in the deepening darkness strangely comforting on the lonely stretch of road with its row of forbidding pine trees.

At last the driver began his move to overtake her. Fleur didn't think a bend in the road was a good place to choose, but the lack of oncoming traffic probably encouraged him.

It had to be a *him*, she reasoned, a woman wouldn't take such a risk. She eased the pressure of her foot on the accelerator and moved over to allow him all the room he might need.

The vehicle drew level. Holding

steady, Fleur glanced sideways. It was a sturdy looking van, but not shiny new, the cabin dark, with not even a cigarette glow to give an indication of its driver. It edged slightly ahead of her but still didn't pass.

Nervously, she wondered what the person was doing. Was he a bad driver? Or did the engine lack power? She slowed still further.

Suddenly the van's nose turned inward, crowding her.

'Maniac!' she shouted, shocked into uncharacteristic anger against the driver. She struggled to control her car as the narrow tarmac gave way to the gravel shoulder and the tyres lost traction. Her outrage turned into a scream as metal screeched against metal, crushing the car door against her right side.

The car slewed sideways towards the deep roadside ditch. Although almost paralysed by fright, she had the sense not to brake hard. She suspected that a sudden halt might cause her vehicle to fishtail or topple.

The front wheels struck the ditch with a bone-jarring jolt that wrenched the steering wheel from her hands. It was not enough to stop the vehicle, nothing could do that. Out of control, it careered towards the looming pine trees.

Some instinct for survival made Fleur put up her arms to shield her face from the inevitable crash.

★ ★ ★

'How are you feeling today?' asked a voice from the end of her hospital bed.

'If only you knew how many times I've already been asked that this morning,' Fleur answered wearily, without opening her eyes. The headache she didn't dare mention wasn't helped by the ward noise. And the interruptions. 'When may I go home?'

'I've come to take you there.'

Her eyelids shot up like spring-loaded roller-blinds.

'How did you know I was in hospital?' she demanded of Lucas Gray.

'It's my job.'

She struggled into a sitting position, one hand going self-consciously to the bandage on her head.

'I take it you're not happy to be here,' he went on. It was more of a statement rather than a question. 'I see you are already dressed . . . ' His eyes took in the plastic bag on the bedside table. 'And packed.'

'I didn't come prepared,' she reminded him. 'I was in an accident.'

He nodded, but said nothing.

'I've been waiting for permission to leave,' Fleur explained, swinging her trousered-legs over the side and finding her sandals.

'There was something about not releasing you until someone responsible was found to escort you.'

'So you are considered someone responsible, are you?' It was a silly remark. The private investigator in his business suit looked the model of responsibility.

'The address of your next-of-kin didn't exactly inspire the hospital with confidence.'

Fleur's heart sank. This was her mother's doing. In a gesture of reconciliation, she had confided in her mother. It was clearly a mistake. Elaine Mitchell obviously didn't understand Lucas had been engaged to find Tom, not to act as a family friend.

'I really am embarrassed, taking you away from your work like this. Perhaps we could go through the motions until we're clear of the hospital, then I could catch a taxi,' she said determinedly.

She stood up. The room spun, and Lucas Gray became a blur, a startled blur that moved quickly to her side.

She sank back on to the edge of the bed again.

'Easy does it,' he murmured, placing a hand firmly under her elbow.

'How silly of me,' she protested, making another effort.

There was no way she was going to stay any longer.

He picked up the small parcel of her belongings. He left one hand where it was, and guided her toward the door and down the corridor to the nurses' station.

Papers signed and farewells said, they crossed the car park to his indistinguishable dark-blue car. Fleur was glad to reach it.

'Where to?' he asked as he slipped behind the wheel.

'I'm surprised you don't know that,' she quipped.

The beginnings of a smile tugged at the corners of his mouth. 'I thought you might have big ideas about how to spend the rest of the day.' The smile got the better of him and became a grin. 'You independent women!' He shook his head in amusement and turned the ignition key.

Fleur gave in to the luxury of being taken care of. She didn't rouse herself until the car slowed to a halt at her front door.

'I don't want you to think I'm

ungrateful, but I'll be all right,' she said, as she fumbled with her keys. 'Some friends are coming in after school.'

He took the bunch of keys from her without a word and, opening the door, followed her inside.

'You just sit down there and I'll make you a cup of tea. If I know anything about hospital routines you will have missed morning tea.'

Fleur didn't object. You can carry independence too far, she decided, easing her bruised body into one of her new leather chairs. It wasn't long before he re-appeared with a tea-tray.

'How's the headache now?' he asked, setting it down.

Fleur was surprised. 'How did you . . . ?' she asked, a little fearful of his powers of observation.

'You've been frowning,' he answered.

She gave a little laugh. 'Much better since leaving the hospital. Everyone was very kind, but I'm not used to . . . to communal living.'

'Then perhaps you'll tell me about

the accident.' He had become the private investigator.

'An idiot ran me off the road. And didn't stop!'

'How do you know that? Your mother said you were found unconscious by a passing motorist, who called the ambulance. What makes you think it couldn't have been the same person?'

Fleur's cup rattled in its saucer. She didn't want to revisit that night, to feel again the waves of conscious pain that gave way to blackouts, the vaguely remembered flashing blue light then sirens and a red light. There were voices and kindly hands, and finally, after a long time, the comfort of a hospital bed.

'It's what I was told,' she said.

'And have you been told the car is a write-off?'

'Yes, but I'm insured.'

Lucas Gray put down his cup and leaned forward, his face serious. 'It would help if I knew what really happened. You are my client, naturally I have an interest in everything you do. It could have a bearing on my enquiries.'

Fleur felt her stomach knot. She knew she had done the wrong thing and should have at least informed him of her own impulsive effort to find Tom. Should she do that now? The idea was swiftly dismissed. He would question her still further and that was the last thing she needed right now.

'I suggest to you someone deliberately pushed you, not ran you off the road,' he went on, rather like a terrier with a bone, she thought. 'There were indentations and traces of cream paint along the driver's side of your car, not consistent with a head-on collision with a tree.'

It was too late to confess. 'Aren't the insurance people satisfied?' she asked.

'Yes, they are. The car was wrecked in an accident caused by an unknown vehicle. They've accepted that and will pay you. But the police are not buying the run-off-the-road theory. Didn't they come and interview you in hospital?'

'Yes, but I told them I couldn't remember much.' A cliché. 'It all happened so quickly,' she added, putting up her hand to her head.

It was enough. The private investigator in Lucas Gray disappeared, replaced by the gentleman he obviously was.

'You must be overtired. I'll leave you now. Are you sure your friends will be in this afternoon? I see there's food in the fridge.'

'Yes, yes.' Fleur smiled. 'My friends . . .'

'I'll go then. Don't get up, I'll see myself out.' He paused at the door and turned. 'Look after yourself,' he said.

★   ★   ★

Fleur woke at first light. She stretched carefully. There was no answering pain. She stretched again, less carefully this time. She smiled. The long sleep in her own bed, uninterrupted by nursing staff on night rounds, had done her good.

It felt good to be in her own bathroom, too. She unwrapped the

44

head bandage, replacing it with a stick-on dressing supplied by the hospital. After a quick brush of her hair and teeth, she grabbed her gown and shrugged herself into it.

While the coffee perked, she continued on to the living-room, pulled back the heavy curtains and looked out.

Wreathed in the last of an overnight mist, the cul-de-sac was quiet. Not even a hum of traffic on the distant freeway reached the house. That had been a plus when she came to buy.

Only one car stood parallel-parked at the kerb opposite.

Fleur turned away.

Something about the car caused her to turn back and look again. Yes, there was a figure slumped in the driver's seat! Her heart skipped a beat. With an effort, she calmed herself.

Why would she assume there was something wrong? Although it was early, it could well be someone waiting to pick up a friend to go to work.

As she watched, the figure moved

and sat up in his seat. A car, a familiar dark-blue car, glided into view, parked and a man, again familiar, got from it.

What was Lucas Gray doing in her street at this time of the morning?

He walked to the first car and bent down to speak to the occupant through the open window. There was a short conversation between the two men, a quick glance toward her house.

Fleur instinctively drew back, flattening herself against the wall, out of sight, her mind jumping to the obvious conclusion. She couldn't believe she had been under surveillance.

It was too late to pretend she was still asleep. She went to the door.

'Coffee, anyone?' she called across the short distance between her and the two men.

Lucas Gray straightened up at the sound of her voice. 'Why, thank you, Fleur.'

The other man got out of his car rather eagerly, Fleur thought. She had sympathy for him. Watching over her all night must've been a bore. But why had Lucas thought it necessary?

'Fleur, this is Wayne. Wayne, Fleur Mitchell.'

The introductions over, Fleur led the way into the kitchen, waving them into chairs whilst she served the coffee.

'This is good coffee,' remarked Wayne, after the first sip.

There was silence. Fleur could think of nothing to say beyond a murmured thank you. Her mind was fixated on the whys and wherefores of the surveillance. And clearly something was bothering Lucas Gray.

Wayne finished his coffee, and pushed back his chair. 'I'll be getting along then,' he said.

Lucas was standing at the bench, helping himself to another cup of coffee when Fleur returned from seeing Wayne to the front door.

'You're looking better this morning.'

There was an air of barely suppressed anger about him, as if he found it hard to be polite.

Fleur's state of undress made her feel vulnerable, she pulled her gown farther across her body and tightened the belt and nodded.

'What were you doing out at Red Hill?' he asked in the same deadly calm voice.

She felt like one of her pupils caught in a misdemeanour. Guilt, and not a little fear of his displeasure, made her respond more defiantly than she intended. Like a pupil.

'Why did you make that poor man spend the night outside my door?' she demanded, going on the offensive. 'I'm all right. I can look after myself.'

'You obviously can't.'

'Anyone can be run off the road by another driver, if that's what you mean. It's one of the hazards of being on the road.'

'You know that's not what I mean.' The piercing blue eyes were trained on her. 'I interviewed your headmaster yesterday.'

4

Fleur tried to shake off a feeling of guilt. There was no reason for her to be that way. After all, Lucas was being employed by her, not the other way around. All she had done was become impatient.

True, having given him the job she should have left all the enquiring to him, but that was no reason for him to react so strongly. Did he dislike any sign of independence in a woman? Was that what this was about?

She decided to ignore his displeasure, hoping Phillip had kept to the known facts about Tom and not mentioned the Vietnam veterans.

'Was he able to help?' she asked. 'With Education Department sources, I mean.'

Lucas' gaze didn't waver. 'Yes, he's given me the name of a colleague in

Records that will save me a lot of time in looking for Tom's home address.'

Fleur breathed a little more easily. She told herself his bad mood probably had to do with something at the office. Or perhaps, like her, he just wasn't good in the mornings. But it still didn't explain Wayne's all-night vigil.

'It was very nice of you to worry about me, but there was no need for Wayne to sit outside all night,' she said.

'He wasn't there all night. He was on the two-to-six shift.'

This was becoming more and more ridiculous. 'Was there someone else earlier?'

'Yes.' His answer dropped like a stone into a deep pool.

'And you were that someone?'

'Yes.'

It didn't make sense. 'I still don't understand the need for you or anyone else to watch over me. It isn't as if I have a life-threatening condition — '

The dam broke, the careful control of the private investigator swept away in a torrent of words. 'No, but you do have a life-threatening situation! Phillip Bennett supplied you with an address at Red Hill. If you had told me you were going there I would have warned you against it. Instead, you blunder in, and look what happened!'

Fleur wrinkled her brow in genuine bewilderment. 'What do you mean, look what happened?' she asked.

'You were run off the road.' His anger disappeared as quickly as it had come. He put a hand on her shoulder and gently pressed her down into a chair, pulling out the one opposite for himself. 'Why don't you tell me what happened?'

It was Fleur's turn to be annoyed. 'How many times do I have to go over this? A bad driver ran me off the road, I lost control of the car. It's as simple as that.'

He leaned forward. 'Fleur, tell me what happened at that farm.'

It didn't take her long. She shivered as she recalled the fierce dogs straining inside the fence, the last of the sun's rays highlighting the barrel of the veteran's gun. Lucas put out a hand to cover her convulsively clenching fists. It encouraged her.

'There was a man . . . with a gun . . . Are you suggesting he came after me?' she asked, her voice a mere whisper of dryness. At last, she was making sense of the private investigator's behaviour. 'And you think he could still come after me? Here?'

Lucas nodded. 'Something like that.'

'It's not possible, he didn't know me. Nor my address. And I was taken directly to hospital, not brought here.' Fleur wished she believed herself, but a part of her allowed for doubt.

'Did you tell him your name?' he asked.

'No, of course not. He thought I was a reporter, but I told him I was a school teacher.' Her hands went up to her lips with a little gasp of realisation. She shook her head. 'No school would give out a teacher's home address, would they?'

'What about the number plate of your car? That information is easy to access if you know how. Did you change your address on your motor registration when you moved?'

'Of course. But it doesn't make sense. Why would he come after me? It isn't as if I had trespassed on to the property. I only drove up to the gate.'

'When you came to me with this enquiry, I warned you we might run into trouble,' Lucas explained. 'There are Vietnam veterans so disaffected by their treatment by society that they have set up us-against-the-world enclaves around the country. That was not an army establishment you went to, it's one of those enclaves. By going there you stirred up an ants' nest.

'I'm hoping they will just scurry around like disturbed ants for a little while and then calm down. They've given you a warning. They might consider that enough, but we can't be sure.'

'What do you suggest? You and Wayne can't sit up all night outside my door.'

'Is there somewhere you can stay for a few days?'

'I can't go home to Mother, if that's what you're suggesting,' Fleur said, managing a ghost of a smile at her wit.

'No-one among your friends?'

'Most are already bunking in.' The thought of even one night in any of the younger teachers' chaotic accommodation was almost worse than the possible threat of a Vietnam veteran finding her. She just had to believe he wouldn't come.

Lucas stood up, breaking the intimacy of the moment. 'I strongly suggest we maintain a watch for a few nights. I should mention this will be an additional expense. I have to ask are you willing to pay that?'

When the decision to find Tom had been made, Fleur had pledged herself not to quibble over the amount she was prepared to spend, even if it meant dipping into her savings. Her impulsiveness had brought about this extra cost. She sighed and nodded.

'Of course, there is another solution, one you might not care for . . . ' Lucas paused. She thought she detected a slight diffidence in his manner. 'You have a spare bedroom.'

'Wayne?' The idea was preposterous. She had only just gained her independence and was enjoying living on her own. Evenings of trying to make conversation with a stranger didn't bear thinking about. 'No!'

Lucas said nothing.

Fleur tried to give an acceptable excuse. 'I don't know him and I'd say we have little in common . . . and I don't believe I'm at any risk — '

There was a stillness about Lucas that made her break off. 'I was going to suggest myself but, as you don't know me either, that would not suit you,' he said.

Confusion sent colour rushing to her cheeks. Her opinion of Wayne, which sounded so snobbish, certainly couldn't be applied to this urbane man.

There was certainly little about her now of the free and easy, flower-power girl Tom had known and loved. In those heady days she would have thrown open her home to anyone, if her mother had allowed it. But the last twenty years had changed her into a very proper school-ma'am, objecting to having a strange man in her house even on business.

* * *

Fleur found she had no need to be anxious about the effect a man would have in her house. She never saw Lucas. No matter how late it was that she went to bed, he was later, almost as if he knew the exact moment.

Invariably, he was gone before her in the morning, his tidy bedroom showing no sign of his being there. There was little evidence of him using the en-suite, either. She wondered when and where he showered, and began to watch for him to develop the unkempt characteristics of an undercover man she'd always expected a private investigator would present.

He certainly was thorough in his job. 'I'll need to use your garage. A car regularly parked outside in the street would be a give-away,' he had said when Fleur agreed to his plans for her safety. Still unconvinced of a threat to her, she had laughed.

'Oh, come on, Lucas, these are the nineteen eighties. The neighbours wouldn't take any notice.'

'The neighbours aren't my worry,' he had reminded her.

Speculation about his private life began to fascinate Fleur. Did he leave her house early and return to some dormitory suburb to shower and have breakfast with a wife and children before beginning a day's work in his office?

5

One morning his routine changed. Sounds of kitchen activity and the smell of coffee and toast greeted Fleur as she emerged from her bedroom dressed for school. The newspaper had been retrieved from the front garden and lay folded beside a place mat on the dining-room table. Butter, marmalade and a glass of orange juice were set out.

Lucas came from the kitchen carrying a rack of toast and a cup of coffee. He looked immaculate as usual, ready for the office.

'Good morning, Fleur,' he said, taking a chair at the opposite end of the table. 'I have something to tell you,' he went on in answer to her quizzical look.

'It must be bad news to warrant this attention,' she said, gesturing toward her breakfast.

Lucas laughed. 'Actually, it's good

news. This is my way of saying I was wrong.'

He became serious. 'The police will be contacting you sometime today. They have traced the van that ran you off the road. The driver was a young man who has lost his licence after several drink-driving convictions and didn't want to be caught out.

'Well, he has been, but not by a breath test. It's too late for that. He'll be charged with driving whilst unlicensed as well as with failure to stop after an accident, although he did call the ambulance from the next town. That's in his favour.'

Never particularly good in the morning, Fleur was slow to react. 'That's in his favour?' she repeated.

'Well, actually, there's nothing in his favour. He shouldn't have been behind the wheel at all, but at least he had the decency not to leave you there.' Lucas' face had darkened.

So had her mood. Favour and decency weren't words she could

associate with the remembered shock of the accident and its consequences. Unable to think straight, she pushed aside her uneaten breakfast and got up.

'I really must go or I'll be late for school,' she muttered.

Lucas stood in her way, determined to have his say. 'This means I was wrong about the threat from the Vietnam veterans.'

Fleur made a gesture of impatience and stepped around him. 'Yes, yes,' she said, gathering her carry-all from where she had thrown it down the night before.

'You'd be quite within your rights to say I told you so,' he said, following her as she snatched up her keys and made for the front door.

'I'm not that kind of person,' she said, turning sharply to protest. Lucas was closer than she expected, his strong body hard up against hers, boxing her in. He didn't move away.

'I know. That was just my little joke.'

He smiled down at her. 'Jokes aren't good in the morning?'

Fleur shook her head faintly, overcome by the sweetness of his smile. He really was a nice man. 'Remembering upsets me,' she explained.

'Do you have to rush off now?' He looked at his watch. 'It's earlier than usual and you've had nothing to eat. I'll make fresh toast and coffee.'

Admitting Lucas was right, that it was still too early for school, Fleur allowed herself to be coaxed back to the table.

She drank the orange juice and let herself relax whilst the unappetising cold toast and coffee were whisked away and, after a short time replaced.

'This toast is very much to my liking,' she commented, reaching for the marmalade. 'Where did you learn your domestic skills? I can't help noticing you're very house-trained. You've been here over a week and I'd hardly know it.'

'I won't have to be here any longer,'

he replied. 'And, because I was wrong, I will not be charging you for my extra time.'

It didn't answer her question. She wondered was that deliberate and tried again.

'You didn't use the shower in the en-suite.'

'My intention was not to make extra work for you,' he said. 'And now, talking of work, I must get on with mine. I'll be in touch as soon as I have something to report. Be patient, it all takes time.'

Fleur couldn't take offence at his gentle rebuff. It was telling her his private life was clearly out of bounds, no business of hers. It was also reminding her that investigating was his business. Again, not hers.

Quite at ease with him, she stood up and, forgetting the half-eaten piece of sticky toast in her hand, followed him to the door. 'I'll not do anything silly,' she promised, putting out the hand to be shaken. 'Goodbye.'

Lucas looked down, his grin widening as Fleur realised her mistake. Walking around with food in her hand! How her table manners had deteriorated since living on her own, without her mother's critical eye. She backed away in embarrassment and closed the door behind her.

★　★　★

It was Sunday and a perfect day for a party. Fleur sat on the floor in a mess of wrappings and house-warming gifts. Through the open doors to the patio the smell of barbecued meat teased the appetite.

She hardly heard the doorbell above the chatter of her friends. Who could it be? She looked around the room. The invited guests were all there.

'I'll go,' offered Camille, getting up out of her chair. 'I'm closest.'

All eyes were on the doorway when she reappeared, the music suddenly loud in the silence that enveloped the room.

'I'm returning your key,' Lucas said, holding it up before placing it in the key-basket on the sideboard and turning to leave.

Fleur felt a rush of warmth to her face and scrambled to her feet, smoothing down her skirt with a nervous gesture. It was hardly the best time for him to choose to return the key. Or to wave it about in front of everybody!

The silence was broken as everyone began chatting again. At that moment, Phillip came in from the patio.

'Oh, hello, Lucas! Good to see you again,' he called cheerfully. 'The meat is ready, Fleur.'

Lucas hesitated long enough to return the headmaster's greeting.

'You'll stay for lunch?' Fleur asked politely, half expecting him to plead commitments elsewhere.

Camille added her invitation, urging him further into the room, clearly impressed by the private investigator's looks. Fleur could see why Lucas would appeal to her thirty-year-old friend.

The business suit gone, he looked good, suitably casual in an open-necked shirt and jeans.

'Thank you very much, Fleur,' he said, his eyes seeking hers. 'I'd like to.'

Fleur hid her surprise and, leaving Camille to look after the newly-arrived guest, turned her attention to organising the food.

Camille burst into the kitchen and came to stand close up to Fleur.

'You didn't tell me he was good looking,' she accused her friend in a low, sibilant voice.

'I hadn't noticed,' Fleur replied truthfully. Not until today, she could have added, surprising herself.

'Don't give me that. You'll have to get over your habit of blushing if you're going to lie.'

'I am not lying. You seem to forget the reason I've engaged Lucas, that is to find Tom, nothing else.'

'If you're not interested then I'm going after him,' Camille retorted.

'He could be married, we don't know.'

Ignoring the warning, Camille took a bowl in each hand and with a confident toss of her head, left the room.

Fleur smiled. Poor Lucas! Camille could be very determined when she set her mind on anything, and that included men. It usually ended with her scaring them off.

Camille's campaign was in full swing when Fleur carried a tray of smaller dishes into the living-room. She could see her friend monopolising Lucas out on the patio. There was no competition from the younger girls. To them anyone over twenty-five was considered old.

'Congratulations on a successful party, my dear,' said Phillip's wife, Barbara. 'I'm so glad you asked us.'

'And I'm glad you were able to come. It's my first, and naturally I was a little nervous.'

'Your new house is ideal for this kind of entertaining,' Barbara went on. 'I'm trying to get Phillip to sell our place and move into something smaller, but he — '

She broke off as the telephone rang. 'Excuse me,' said Fleur, picking up the cordless receiver and walking out on to the patio for privacy. Lucas' eyes met hers over Camille's shoulder. She wondered was it in desperation of amusement.

The caller identified herself. It was the retirement village's weekend supervisor. Without breaking the glance between herself and Lucas, Fleur felt for a chair and sank into it, expecting a lengthy conversation about minor matters.

The message was brief and to the point.

Lucas was at her side in an instance. 'What is it?' he asked.

'My mother has had a fall and been admitted to hospital.'

6

Unable to supply Lucas with any more than the barest details as she knew them, Fleur lapsed into silence in the car, her mind busy. The supervisor of the retirement village had offered no explanation for her mother's fall.

It didn't make sense, she'd been walking less and less and spending more and more time in her wheelchair over the past year. Did this mean she'd fallen out of it?

Lucas drove confidently through the light Sunday traffic until they reached the distant suburb and the major hospital.

There was a sameness about the atmosphere there that reminded Fleur unhappily of her own recent stay in hospital. And of how lucky she'd been to escape serious injury in the crash.

Walking patients and anxious relatives thronged the heavily-signposted foyer, and she was glad to have Lucas do her thinking for her. His hand at her back directed her through the crowd.

'I'll wait for you in the visitors' lounge,' he said tactfully at the door of her mother's private room in the orthopaedic wing.

'There's no need for you . . . ' she began, but he was already striding back down the corridor. Fleur wanted to say that she appreciated his help but didn't expect him to give up a Sunday barbecue.

Camille certainly hadn't been happy about it, judging by the look of frustration on her friend's face when Lucas, without a moment's hesitation, made his offer to drive to the hospital.

Her face pinched with pain, Elaine Mitchell lay with one leg encased in a temporary cradle-cast and elevated on a pile of pillows.

'Oh, there you are at last,' she

exclaimed, her voice loaded with accusation.

'I came as soon as I got word,' Fleur replied, still thinking of the guests she'd left. Fortunately, Camille was well able to look after them. 'What happened?'

'It's your fault, telling me to walk more.'

Fleur sighed. 'I just repeated your doctor's orders,' she gently reminded her mother. 'It's a good thing you chose today and not a school day. I was only having a house-warming party,' she went on, trying to jolly her mother. 'Now, how did this happen? What's the diagnosis? Is it serious? I should go and ask the doctor first, and then you can tell me all about it, how it happened.'

Her mother objected to her leaving. 'You just got here. I'm in pain.'

'I'll see to that, too,' Fleur replied patiently, giving up her attempt to lighten her mother's mood. She had cried wolf so often in the past it was hard for Fleur to know how serious the injury was. 'I'll only be a moment.'

She was wrong about that. It took more than a moment to learn her mother had fractured an ankle and that it would require pinning as soon as the swelling went down. It also took time to have a request for painkillers authorised. And finally, to locate Lucas.

The visitors' lounge at the far end of the corridor was a haven of quietness, the private investigator its only occupant. He sat upright on the couch, hands clasped loosely on the open magazine in his lap, his eyes closed. She listened to his rhythmic breathing, reluctant to wake him.

Not for the first time Fleur wondered about his life. She knew she wouldn't be his only client, his offices told her that it was a successful business. And by its very nature, it wasn't a nine-to-five job. Snatched sleep would be a part of the job requirements.

'Lucas,' she called softly.

He was alert instantly, and on his feet.

'It looks as if I'll be here a while, my

mother is not settling too well,' she told him. 'Thank you for bringing me, I really appreciated it.'

He brushed aside her thanks. Taking a pen and a business card from the top pocket of his jacket, he scribbled a number on it. 'Here's my private number. Call me when you're ready to go home, no matter what the time, and I'll come and get you,' he instructed, handing it to her.

'No, no, I can't have you driving back and forth all night. I'll take a taxi.' Fleur's protests were overridden by his stern look. 'This is going far beyond your duty to a client,' she ended meekly.

'It's all part of the service,' he replied, a sudden smile changing his face. 'Now, call me!'

And when the time came, she did.

The return journey through the empty streets to her home seemed to take no time at all. After bringing Lucas up-to-date with her mother's condition, she thankfully sank back into the comfortable seat.

She stole a look at his profile. How easily he had fitted into her world. She wondered if he was like that with all his clients.

Lucas brought the car to a standstill in front of her house. Camille had thoughtfully left a welcoming porch light burning. Fleur knew all traces of the party would be gone, too, and the house returned to order. Camille was good like that.

'I'll walk you to the door,' Lucas said, getting out and coming to the passenger side.

'There's very little of the night left, would you like to . . . ? Your bed . . . the spare bed is made up . . . ' Fleur couldn't believe what a mess she was making of a very simple offer. It had been a day of drama, beginning with his arrival at the barbecue and she wasn't thinking clearly. 'It would save you a lot of driving,' she said.

'Thanks, Fleur, but it's not much further to the office — '

'The office? But that's in the city.'

'Yes.'

She waited for him to say something more, but as the moment stretched into a minute, and he said goodnight, she realised he wasn't going to supply her with details of his private life.

* * *

In the week that followed, Fleur forgot her quibbles over the private investigator and his determinedly private life. She mentally consigned him to Camille as she struggled to cope with school and visits to the hospital. At last her mother's injury was pronounced operable and Fleur took the day off to be with her.

At first, the pre-theatre preparation did little to calm Elaine Mitchell's nervousness, but by the time the wardsmen came to wheel her down the long corridors, the medication was beginning to take effect. Fleur noticed her voice fading, her sentences becoming disjointed.

'You're not going to Sydney, are you?' her mother asked in the lift.

'Sydney? Why would I be going to Sydney?' Fleur bent low over the trolley hoping to catch the answer. 'I'm staying right here with you,' she said reassuringly, squeezing her mother's hand.

'Sydney . . . Tom . . . '

Sydney? Where had that idea come from?

Consumed by curiosity, Fleur wanted to ask her mother what she meant, but it was too late. They were out of the lift and had reached the doors to the operating suite.

A team of assistants came forward to claim their patient.

'You'll have to go now, Miss Mitchell. Don't worry, we'll look after your mother,' promised the leader.

But, as she told Lucas when he rang for a progress report some days later, her mother had no recollection of saying anything about Sydney or Tom. No amount of questioning could sway her.

'The nursing staff tell me it's the effect of the anaesthetic. It wipes out memory.'

'Drugs or not, your mother may unwittingly have given us a clue which, without the operation, might never have come out.'

He'd correctly summed up her mother. Elaine Mitchell certainly wouldn't willingly help to find Tom, even if she did remember her subconscious remark. She'd been against Fleur searching for him from the start.

'Why would you waste time and money doing that?' she'd asked when Fleur told her of her intentions.

'Because I want to put it right,' Fleur had stubbornly replied. Even after twenty years, Tom needed to know he hadn't been deserted. He deserved it.

Lucas went on. 'I think notices in the Sydney newspapers asking for information might bring a response. I'm certainly drawing a blank through the normal channels and before this, had been considering widening the enquiry to include the national newspapers. Some relative, or perhaps another veteran might give us a clue.'

7

Fleur hadn't dreamed it would be so difficult to find Tom, although both the Vietnam Veterans' Association and Lucas had warned her of the certain percentage of veterans who didn't want to be found. Perhaps Tom was among them.

She comforted herself with the knowledge that at least he hadn't been killed, or listed as missing-in-action. Lucas had been able to access Army records and assured her Tom's name was not on either list.

It was after her mother had been moved to a rehabilitation centre for physiotherapy that Lucas rang her.

'I've had a reply to my advertisement — '

'From Tom?' Fleur broke in eagerly, buoyed by the possibility that the search was over.

'Well, it would seem so — '

She cut him off again with another question, apprehension giving an edge to her voice. 'What do you mean, it would seem so?'

'I've had a letter from someone purporting to be Tom Drysdale.' His careful choice of words injected a note of caution into the conversation that worried Fleur.

'I'll know his handwriting,' she assured Lucas.

'It's not handwritten,' he went on.

Fleur felt her heart sink. 'I'll know by what he says,' she insisted, unwilling to give up hope.

'We have to be sure this is our man,' he patiently explained. 'There are people out there who see these advertisements as a chance to make some money.'

'How could anyone be thinking about money? I just want to find him.'

There was a pause before Lucas spoke again. 'Fleur, you've never told me why you want to find Tom. I think you should do that now. It would help if I knew.'

A perverse reluctance took hold of her. She knew little about him, so why should she tell him all her family secrets. Especially now that Tom had been found. That was what he'd been hired for, after all, not to hear what her mother had done.

Fleur said nothing.

'Look, perhaps I should come around,' he suggested in the silence. 'Is it convenient?'

* * *

There was little of Tom in the letter he brought. It was brief, giving details of a Sydney post office box, nothing more, not even a contact telephone number. Fleur could see why Lucas had reservations.

'Confidence men are quick to assume these notices are inserted in the papers by probate lawyers,' he said.

'How can we be sure, then?'

'I'll write to set up a meeting,' he replied, pocketing the letter. 'It'll probably be at least a week before we can expect him to contact me back,' he added, answering her unasked question.

Suddenly, the dream was alive again. But a week? Fleur wondered how she could contain herself.

'How hard is it for you to get leave?' Lucas asked.

'Get leave? What for?'

He gave her a long, hard look. 'I'll need you to confirm this person's identity,' he replied rather formally at last.

Had excitement dulled her brain? Of course she would want to go to Tom just as soon as he replied to Lucas, and that would mean time off work. It went without saying, didn't it? But talking about confirming this person's identity, as he put it, reminded her that to Lucas it was an assignment, presumably about to be brought to a satisfactory conclusion.

8

With her hands wrapped around a long, cool drink, Fleur sat in the comfort of the mezzanine lounge of their Sydney hotel. From there she had a good view of Lucas in a secluded corner of the foyer below, seemingly absorbed in his newspaper.

He had expressed doubts about the true identity of the letter-writer who claimed to be Tom and warned her against getting her hopes too high. She tried not to, but each time the uniformed doorman stepped forward to hold back the heavy glass door, her heart gave a lurch. Each time she was disappointed.

Anticipation of this moment had been building for days, ever since Lucas gave her details of the planned meeting. It increased dramatically during their morning flight from Melbourne, only temporarily lulled by the sight of the beautiful harbour city beneath the wings as the plane came in to land.

Once again, she'd been glad of Lucas' guidance as they made the trip from the airport to the four-star hotel and booked in.

After lunch, he had suggested she rest in her room until the late afternoon meeting, but lying on the bed staring at the ceiling had done little to calm her excitement. If anything, it had increased the tension.

She took another gulp of her drink, and dabbed her lips nervously with a paper serviette.

The foyer became more crowded as the business day ended, with groups of men passing through on the way to the bar. Eventually, a lone figure was directed to the corner where Lucas sat.

Fleur leaned forward, eager for her first glimpse of Tom.

Even allowing for the passage of twenty years, she could see it was not him. This man was shorter, the shape of his head different. There was nothing of her remembered love about the stranger joining Lucas and shaking his hand.

A wave of bitter disappointment swamped Fleur. She sank back into the deep armchair, fighting the tears that obscured her view of the two men. She hardly noticed the drink waiter beside her until he murmured for the second time, 'Another, Madam?'

She nodded mutely, hiding her face.

The tears had been wiped away by the time he returned. She sat up straight in the chair, gave the room number and signed the check, in control of herself again.

Her mind was racing. If this stranger wasn't Tom, who was he? There had to be a connection. Did he know Tom? Or his whereabouts? Was he trying a scam or merely acting on Tom's behalf? If the latter, why hadn't he said so in his letter?

An idea was hatching. Whatever his motive, he could lead them to Tom. She corrected herself. Lead her. Lucas was already known to him, but she wasn't. There was no likelihood he could identify her even if he had seen a twenty-year-old photo that had been carried into the steamy jungles of Vietnam.

Without stopping to consider that Lucas may already know the man's identity, and it might not be necessary, Fleur made up her mind to follow him.

Leaving her unfinished drink, she gathered up her bag and calmly walked down the wide staircase into the crowded lobby. Because the reception desk was in clear view of both men, she decided it was too risky to leave a message for Lucas. The man might notice and remember her later.

As for Lucas, his all-seeing, all-knowing eyes would immediately suspect she was about to break her promise not to do anything without his approval.

Fleur consoled herself this was an exception and that he might come to thank her afterwards. She chose a chair close to the door but hidden from both men, and sat down to wait.

At last the stranger accepted a card from Lucas and after shaking hands, walked across the foyer toward her. Fleur searched his face again in a vain hope her memory may have tricked her, but there was definitely nothing of Tom about him.

She slipped past the doorman and out into the street. Homeward-bound crowds made it easy to follow the man closely without raising his suspicions. Before long he turned in at a nearby railway station entrance.

Dismayed, Fleur hesitated. When she made the decision to follow the man she hadn't considered the possibility of a rail journey. Could she keep him in sight?

She hoped he needed to buy a ticket, too, but he went with the flow and, fishing in his pocket for what she imagined was a pass, headed for the turnstiles.

Fuming at the enforced delay, Fleur

pushed a twenty-dollar note in at the ticket-office window, her eyes on her quarry. The peak-hour press of people had formed a bottle-neck but was still carrying him slowly away from her.

If the clerk didn't hurry with her ticket it was possible he could be swallowed up by the crowd, or if a train came in before she reached him, be lost to her altogether.

The ticket-seller asked for a destination. She hadn't thought of that, either.

'End of the line,' she answered, taking her eye off the man for a moment to lean up close to the grille, almost shouting in her impatience.

'Which line?'

She stared at him blankly through the bars. How would she know that? The system was totally unknown to her. With a shrug that said he wasn't prepared to waste time with her, the clerk punched out a ticket.

Change clattered into the outlet. Fleur swiped up the ticket and some of the money and raced toward the turnstiles, ignoring the shout from the next customer. She hoped she'd left behind enough to buy them a ticket.

The silver train slid into the platform just as Fleur wormed her way into a position beside the impostor, for that was how she was thinking of him. Carried forward by the pressure of the crowd, they surged through the doors together.

As the doors closed and the train moved off, she stared at the stranger and once again reassured herself it was not Tom. Her memory of him could not be that far astray.

She could feel her knees weakening as the enormity of what she was doing engulfed her. She was on a train in a strange city, going she knew not where, following a man not known to her. It was a far cry from her normal teacher's life.

At each station there was a shifting of passengers as some left the train. Seats at the far end of the carriage became vacant, but she daren't take one. Afraid the stranger might leave the train if her attention wavered, Fleur clung to the overhead strap, swaying under the movement, willing her legs not to give way under her.

The view from the train changed as treed suburban backyards took the place of city buildings and factories. The carriage was emptying the farther it went, but the man showed no sign of leaving.

He chose one of the vacant seats and sat down.

Fleur's heart sank. How far into the suburbs was he leading her? It would take forever to return to the city, but she couldn't give up now. Knowing she would draw attention to herself if she remained standing, she slid into a space opposite him.

Looking at his perfectly normal, everyday face, a paranoid thought entered her mind. If this man was trying to pull off a scam by pretending to be Tom, he wasn't going about it in a furtive manner. That meant he was confident. And clever.

But couldn't that also mean he was aware she was following him? Was he drawing her out to the end of the line to leave her stranded? That certainly would be clever. A woman alone, at night . . .

Quickly she put an end to that idea. It was not something she wanted to think about. She had to believe he didn't suspect her or give up the chase. The train slowed for another station and quite a few passengers, including her man, prepared to alight.

There was a moment of hesitation when her courage could easily have evaporated. What was she doing? Had her good sense deserted her? Following this man had seemed like a good idea at the time but was she meddling in something she knew nothing about?

There was a good chance he was a Vietnam veteran. The warning sound of doors about to close made the decision for her. Spurred into action, she dived through the narrowing opening and stepped off the train.

9

Outside the station the group of alighting passengers scattered. Fleur's next concern was that the impostor might get into one of the vehicles in the station car-park, but he crossed it on foot and turned into a side street.

She found she was one of several people on the street. In typical big-city fashion, no-one spoke to anyone else. All thoughts of the man being aware of her had gone. She became just another anonymous homecoming householder.

There were still people in the street when the stranger suddenly stopped at the gate of an ordinary suburban house, and opened it. He bent to check the letter-box before continuing up the path to the front door.

The momentary pause at the gate meant Fleur had overtaken him. There was nothing she could do but walk on by, racking her brains as to what to do next.

She hadn't thought past following him, despite having plenty of time on the outward journey to make contingency plans. What a private eye she'd make!

It was Lucas' job to take this farther. She would make a note of the address and catch the train back to the city. She hoped they ran frequently. She didn't like the idea of hanging about a deserted railway station once night came. There was no way of knowing how safe it was after peak-hour.

Now nervousness of another kind overtook her. She became impatient to return and tell Lucas what she had discovered. He'd be surprised. It was so unlike her to do anything so impulsive but surely he would be pleased with the information she was bringing. This man, whoever he was, obviously was a con-artist.

The short street ended abruptly in a court with no through-way, presenting her with a new dilemma. How was she going to walk back past his house?

Desperately, she looked for a solution. Nearby, a real estate sign announced a house for sale. If anyone was watching it could be her reason for being there!

Confidence restored, she stopped, took her address book from her bag and pretended to give the sale house a detailed inspection, then turned away.

In the fading light she hurried in the direction of the station, without wondering why his approval or disapproval mattered.

★ ★ ★

Lucas was impatiently pacing the foyer, at the same time trying hard not to look conspicuous. Fleur pushed through the hotel's heavy glass door.

'Where have you been? Was it Tom?' His voice had a rough edge to it that surprised her.

She looked for an empty chair and

sank into it, suddenly aware of a dryness in her mouth. 'May I have a drink first? Just water, please.'

He signalled the waiter, made the request and sat down beside her.

'Well, was it Tom?' he asked, more gently this time.

She shook her head.

'I thought not.'

They sat in silence until the drink came, and she quenched her thirst.

'I'm sorry, Fleur,' he said as he took the empty glass from her hand. 'What happened to you?'

The gentle question almost undid her. She struggled with an almost overwhelming desire to seek the comfort of his arms and let go of the delayed tears of disappointment that were building up behind her eyes. It would be so good for her but the hotel foyer was not the place to break down. Lucas wouldn't appreciate it — no man would.

'Do you mind if I tell you about it at dinner? I'd like to freshen up,' she replied, surprised at the steadiness of her voice.

To Fleur's relief, Lucas was not overly critical of her actions when she met him for dinner in the hotel later that evening. He expressed concern at the risks she'd taken, but commended her for her initiative.

'I'll have to offer you a partnership,' he laughed, his eyes alight with admiration, then became more serious. 'This is not the address the fellow gave,' he mused, comparing her offering with the information he had written in his notebook. 'There's something not quite right about him that I couldn't put my finger on. I wonder who he is and what he's up to.'

'Why would he be pretending to be Tom?' Fleur asked.

Elbows on the table, Lucas rested his chin on his interlocked hands, his forehead creased in concentration. It was a pose becoming familiar to Fleur.

'As I told you, he may have seen an opportunity to make some money, mistaking my advertisement for that of a probate solicitor's. It was hard to tell. He'll need to know a lot about Tom to pull it off.'

A cold hand clutched at her heart as another possible scenario came to mind. 'Probate? You don't think he knows Tom's . . . ' She could hardly bring herself to say the words. ' . . . not coming back?'

'Not necessarily,' Lucas replied quickly. 'We know Tom disappeared after he was discharged here in Australia. He could have asked this fellow to front up on his behalf.'

'But why would he do that?'

'That's something we'll have to find out, isn't it?' He half-turned in his chair to allow the waiter to place his meal in front of him. 'This looks good. I'm hungry.'

'So am I.' said Fleur.

There was silence as they began to eat.

'What will you do next?' she asked, after the edge had been taken off her appetite.

'Tomorrow, I'll check the address he gave me, but until then I intend to enjoy this meal and perhaps go on the harbour. It's a beautiful night for it. What are your plans?'

Fleur looked across the table. Was Lucas asking her to go out with him? She didn't know. Suddenly she felt tired, exhausted by the emotional let-down of believing she was going to see Tom, and the disappointment, followed by the adrenalin rush of tracking the impostor.

'You feel let down,' Lucas remarked when she didn't reply. 'It's been a long and eventful day.'

'Yes, I'm very tired. Would you excuse me?'

Lucas stood up with her. 'See you at breakfast. Sleep well.'

But, despite her tiredness, Fleur did not fall asleep easily. She lay in the darkness of the hotel room, her mind on a merry-go-round of twenty-year-old memories.

She knew when she began looking for

Tom that it would probably be painful, but the need to right the wrong her mother had done had become an obsession. She nursed an unspoken belief that the years of loss could somehow be wiped out once she found him.

Today, despite Lucas' warning, she had hoped the search was over.

Still wide awake after a restless couple of hours, she got up and stepped out on to the balcony.

Voices and laughter reached her from the street below, carried upwards on the velvety night air.

She leaned over the railings, envying the carefree groups spilling out of the hotel. If things had gone right this day as she'd hoped, and the stranger had been Tom, perhaps they would have been part of the ceaseless night life of Kings Cross.

'Fleur?'

She started and turned away from the railings, automatically putting up a hand to check the top button of her robe. Lucas loomed from the darkness of his room and stood by the low dividing fence between the two balconies. In the reflected light from the hotel's illuminations she could see he was still dressed, although coatless.

'Can't you sleep?'

She shook her head, not trusting herself to speak, brought perilously close to tears by the hint of sympathy in his voice.

He put one hand on the low balustrade and vaulted over, covering the distance between them in a stride.

The neon sign changed from red to blue, bathing his face in a cold, hard light. It was the best thing that could have happened as it stopped her tears.

'You thought we'd found Tom, didn't you? Despite my warning that we mightn't?'

The sign flashed back to red, suffusing Lucas with a soft glow. Vulnerable, she wondered was the regret on his face just a trick of the light?

'I was afraid of that.' The tone of his voice was almost tender. It brought her tears close to the surface again. Her lips quivered.

For one wild moment she thought he was going to take her in his arms, but instead, he pulled up one of the outdoor chairs and encouraged her to sit down.

'Why don't you wait here whilst I make us some tea,' he suggested before disappearing into her room.

Glad of the half-dark that hid her foolishness, she watched through the sliding door as he opened the hospitality cupboard and set the electric jug to boil.

He straddled a chair facing her, his face in the shadow as the changing light played against the walls behind him and the white of his business shirt. Soft, harsh, which was the real Lucas Gray?

'How was the harbour trip?' she asked, sipping her tea.

'I didn't go after all. It's not the sort of thing you do on your own. I belong to a club in Melbourne with affiliations with one here. I went there. They have an excellent billiard room.'

Fleur was surprised. 'You don't strike me as the sort of person to hang around clubs.' Despite herself, there was a note of disapproval in her voice that sounded like her mother.

Lucas laughed heartily. 'Your sheltered life is showing, Fleur. Not all clubs are dens of iniquity. This one is quite exclusive. I'll take you there if you like.'

Fleur could feel the flush racing up her neck. It didn't help that he was right about her life up until now. It had been what most people would call, sheltered.

'We won't still be here tomorrow night, will we?' she asked, hoping to divert him. It worked.

'I intend to check out our man at the address he has given me. It will be interesting to see what we discover.'

'I want to come with you, in case Tom's there,' she said.

'Of course you do, and I need you.' He got up from the chair. 'I plan on an early start so we'd better get some rest. Goodnight, Fleur.'

She watched him vault back on to his balcony, then swing around to face her, as if he'd had an afterthought.

'We could stay another night, and go on the harbour, if you wish,' he suggested.

'Not if we find Tom,' she reminded him quickly, believing they would.

'No, of course not,' he replied, before disappearing into his room.

10

The next day began with another disappointment for Fleur. After an early breakfast in the hotel, Lucas called for a taxi that took them a short distance into the Central Business District.

'Is this the address he gave?' she asked, tilting her head back to gaze up at the tall building.

Lucas clearly was not pleased. 'Yes,' replied, tersely, his face set. He put a hand under her elbow and directed her into the lift lobby, along with the stream of office workers.

She wondered what it was like to disappear with hundreds of others into one of these skyscrapers every morning. Rather soul-destroying, she imagined.

'What floor are we looking at?' she asked, running her eyes down the imposing list of companies.

'He didn't say.'

She twisted her head sideways to look at his face, and decided it wasn't a good time to be asking obvious questions. A cold shiver of foreboding dampened down her anticipation. The day was not starting out too well.

At Lucas' request, the concierge behind the enquiry desk looked for Tom's name in his directory.

'I have no listing of anyone of that name working in the building,' he announced. 'Perhaps he's a new employee,' he added. 'Do you have the name of the company? That would be helpful.'

Shaking his head, Lucas turned away from the desk and faced Fleur, his face cleared of whatever frustration he'd been feeling.

'It looks like the trip on the harbour will have to be a daytime one,' he smiled.

Numbed by yet another let-down, Fleur wasn't able to pick up on his meaning.

'Sorry?'

'As I suspected, this is a dead-end. Even if we sat here for hours, I doubt he'd show. This was probably an address chosen off the top of his head when I asked about his workplace.'

Out on the street, he caught the eye of a taxi-driver about to pull away from the kerb and handed her into the cab.

'We'll have to waylay our imposter at his home this evening. In the meantime, I suggest we find something to do until then. What about a cruising lunch?' He raised an eyebrow. 'Circular Quay,' Lucas instructed the taxi-driver.

★   ★   ★

The morning rush of city workers was obviously over, and the first of the tourists were thronging the quays, the speciality shops already busy. With the backdrop of ferries and the sparkling harbour, it was a colourful scene.

'Will you wait here whilst I make enquiries about bookings and sailings?'

Lucas asked and strode off across the forecourt.

Fleur chose a bench opposite a well-stocked flower stall, a perfumed oasis in the city.

'Would you like me to tell your future, dear?' a voice called from the shadowy doorway of a nearby shop that advertised palm readings. An old woman emerged.

At first glance, it was impossible to guess the woman's age, although her clothes and the strong scent of lavender as she sat down suggested another era.

'Give me something of yours to hold.'

Fleur tried not to laugh. It was the oldest trick in the trade and here was a very old trickster trying to pull it off. She shook her head.

'I have psychic powers as well. Just let me hold your hand,' the old woman suggested.

Feeling sorry for her, Fleur decided that although she didn't believe in such things, it wouldn't hurt to humour the old woman. She put out a hand, keeping her handbag close to her body on the off-side.

With eyes closed, the fortune-teller began speaking. 'You've been very lonely, but all that is going to change. You're going to find true happiness.' She opened here eyes and peered closely at Fleur. 'Soon,' she insisted emphatically.

Fleur knew she couldn't take it seriously, but some part of her wanted to believe the prophecy was true. There had been set-backs in the search for Tom and this morning was yet another. She was beginning to doubt they'd ever find him.

It wasn't as if Lucas hadn't tried. What he had said that first day in his office was that some veterans did not want to be found. They had chosen to drop out of the mainstream of life and that could easily apply to Tom.

She lifted her eyes to gaze across the concourse. Lucas was at the flower stall, making a purchase. He came towards her as she watched, carrying a single flower.

'I thought you needed cheering up,' he said, handing it to her. 'It isn't over yet, you know.'

'Aha,' said a knowing voice beside her. 'See? I told you so.'

Fleur laughed, her optimism restored. It was the wrong man, but a good omen. As he said, the search wasn't over yet.

She thanked Lucas, bringing the carnation to her nose and inhaling its musky scent.

'That was very nice of you,' she said. 'But this person probably deserves it more. Do you mind?' She turned to the old woman. 'Thank you,' she said, presenting her with the flower.

It was accepted, but not without a final reminder of the future. 'Soon,' the soothsayer insisted.

11

'What was that all about?' Lucas asked as they walked towards the ferries.

Fleur hesitated. Would he scoff the idea of her taking notice of such an unprepossessing figure? She knew so little about him, apart from his almost old-fashioned courtesy. Did he have a sense of humour?

She wondered if Camille would know the answer to that, but since her mother's accident there had been little time to catch up with her friend. There had only been snatched conversations in the corridors between classes, no chance of an exchange of personal confidences.

Had she and Lucas been seeing each other? Somehow Fleur didn't think so. She knew that Camille would've found a way to tell her if they had.

Deciding not to confide in Lucas, she

laughed. 'Just a funny old lady who took a fancy to me.'

'Why doesn't that surprise me?'

'Sorry?'

No it was his turn to dismiss the remark with an airy wave of his hand. 'Here we are,' he said as they reached the large vessel moored at the jetty.

'This is a wonderful idea of yours, Lucas,' she remarked over her shoulder, leading the way up the gangplank and into the boarding lounge. Through the plate-glass windows, she could glimpse the immediate harbour and the commuter ferries coming into the quay.

Lured by the activity, Fleur took her welcoming drink out on to the open deck. Beneath her feet the engines throbbed gently.

'I've booked our table,' Lucas said, coming to join her at the rails. 'We should be casting off soon.'

Like everything he did, Lucas had chosen well. The table by the windows gave them a clear view of the main harbour, the Opera House and the

Harbour Bridge, the giant coathanger of steel for which the city was renowned.

And the buffet was a delight of gourmet food, with Sydney rock oysters, succulent baked fish and a wide selection of hot dishes and market-fresh salads. Fleur expressed her thanks to Lucas for the experience.

'Do you come to Sydney often?' she asked Lucas. 'You seem to know your way around.'

'My work often brings me here, but I like it for a break as well. It's a real holiday city.'

'For a sophisticated single person, yes, but wouldn't Queensland be a better family destination?' she asked.

In an instant, Fleur knew she'd made a mistake. This was getting too personal. There was a pause before he answered her. 'I have no family.'

'You have no family?' she repeated idiotically. 'I just assumed . . . ' She stopped. Could she say what she was thinking? 'I just assumed when you

111

weren't overly interested in Camille it must've been because you were married . . . '

His eyes smiled. 'I was once, a long time ago, but marriage and this job . . . ' he shrugged. 'And as for your friend, she is a pleasant person, but not my type.'

Emboldened, Fleur asked, 'What is your type? Younger women?'

He didn't seem offended. In fact, the smile extended to a wide grin. 'That would be telling, wouldn't it? You'd bring out some of your young teacher friends and I've never have a moment's peace.'

Their laughter bridged the awkwardness she felt.

The Captain's commentary had concluded and the vessel was nearing the quay before Fleur remembered the reason for their visit to Sydney.

Toying with her teaspoon, she brought the conversation around to the imposter they were about to unmask.

'Why would he give you a bogus

work address, Lucas?'

'I think he realised I was on to him during the interview and this was his way of backing out. I only have a box number as a postal address, so he thinks he can safely disappear back into the woodwork.'

He grinned. 'Of course he doesn't know I have a secret weapon, an eager beaver of an assistant and we — '

'We know where he lives,' Fleur finished the sentence, proudly matching his grin. 'What is the plan, Chief?' she asked.

Their laughter died as Lucas became the private investigator again.

'First things first,' he said, indicating the Rental Car office on the quay below.

∗   ∗   ∗

Fleur was finding it hard to control her excitement. The cruise had been a welcome respite, but confronting the man who had raised, then dashed her hopes, had become her number one priority.

They were in place in the carpark well ahead of the first of the home-coming workers who emerged from the station. As the frequency of the peak-hour trains increased, the tension in the car built until, at last, a familiar figure emerged from the building and began to cross the car-park.

Adrenalin shot through Fleur. She readied herself and put her hand on the door-handle, her eyes focused on Lucas, waiting his word.

'No, not yet. He could get away from us here. Let's follow him home,' he said quietly. 'One at a time, you go first. What I want you to do is go to the front door.'

One at a time? You go first? Suddenly, her excitement had become trepidation.

He stopped. 'You can do it,' he added reassuringly. 'I need to go to the back door in case he realises the game's up and makes a dash for it. OK?'

Fleur wasn't sure what she'd thought would happen, she hadn't got that far in her thinking. Perhaps a polite exchange at the front door? How naive can you get? She asked herself. This was a man who was desperate enough to lie to extract money under false pretences.

That was an illegal act and he would know it. If he came out the back door in a hurry, it would need an experienced man to stop him, not a female school-teacher.

She nodded, her mouth too dry to speak.

'You can do it,' he repeated as he leaned across her to open the car door to let her out.

For a moment she felt the strength of his firm body and, in the welter of emotions she was feeling, pitied the imposter if he tried to get past Lucas.

'Good luck,' he said as he kissed her cheek then straightened up.

For a moment she was unable to move, caught unawares by the touch of his lips, but, with a gentle push, he reminded her of the task ahead. She left the car and followed the imposter in a re-run of the previous night's adventure.

There was no need to panic about keeping him in sight; she knew where he lived this time.

And Lucas was with her.

The man followed the same routine. Fleur slowed to allow him time to check out the letterbox, examine the mail and disappear into the house, then quickened her pace.

With a glance over her shoulder, she checked that Lucas was now close behind her at the edge of the property. He gave the thumbs-up sign of encouragement and vaulted the fence, disappearing into the untidy garden.

Fleur rang the doorbell, setting off a well-known melody she was too nervous to identify. A dog began barking in a distant room, then was suddenly on the other side of the door.

The deep-chested bark told her this

was no lap-dog. She thought of the Vietnam Veterans' enclave with its Doberman dogs and hoped the security door was strong enough to protect her.

A voice called on the dog to quieten down and the door was opened by a teenage girl, still in a school uniform, a restraining hand on the German Shepherd's collar.

'May I speak with your parents?' Fleur asked, warily watching the animal.

Without leaving, the girl turned and shouted down the hallway. 'Mum, someone wants to talk to you,' then returned to her insolent inspection of Fleur's clothes.

A middle-aged woman appeared in the hallway, pushing some order into her greying hair as she came towards the door. 'Yes?'

For a moment Fleur hesitated. How could this ordinary-looking woman in this everyday Australian household be involved in a case of deception? Searching for an answer, she seized on the idea that the wife possibly wasn't aware of her husband's criminal intent.

'I'd like to speak with your husband,' she said.

'Why, yes, I'll get him. Can I tell him what it's about? He's just home from work.'

She might as well have added the words and he's not in a very good mood. It was inferred by her anxious attitude.

'I want to ask him about Tom Drysdale.'

Fleur's judgement of the woman in front of her as possibly an innocent in the attempted fraud was shot to pieces. The housewife visibly started, the colour drained from her face, her eyes widened in dismay.

'Frank,' she called over her shoulder in an agonised voice.

12

The woman's cry put to flight Fleur's idea this was a happy suburban household. Fascinated, she watched the females shrink back against the wall as, bristling with aggression, the impostor appeared at the end of the hallway.

'What?' he demanded,

The girl scuttled away, leaving the dog unrestrained. Barking, it lunged against the security-door. Although she knew it couldn't reach her, Fleur leapt back in alarm, narrowly missing a potted plant.

Lucas hadn't told her of the risks of being a private investigator.

Had she been naïve to imagine it was just a matter of knocking on the front door and politely unmasking the impostor? The short answer was yes.

The man strode toward her, menace in every line of the body no longer clothed in a business suit. There was something about his attitude that was more than the male of the species defending his family with the aid of a guard dog.

Fleur recognised it as a veteran's response to an invasion of his territory. She had seen it before, on the farm at Red Hill.

'What's going on?' he asked belligerently.

'This woman is asking about Tom,' his wife replied.

Escape! Was written all over his face as he turned back. It was too late. Lucas stood in his way.

'What do you think you're doing?'

'Control that dog and let my partner in,' Lucas ordered, not taking his eyes off the man. My partner! Fleur felt a flush of pleasure that was quickly replaced by fear.

Did Lucas have a gun to reinforce his demands? She hoped not. Violence wasn't what she'd had in mind when she began to look for Tom.

To her surprised the man obeyed the authoritive tone, reaching for a dog's leash and muzzle that hung on the hallstand. A cold shiver ran through her body at the implication of the animal's dangerous nature.

'Get rid of it,' said Lucas, still in military mode. The man responded almost automatically, fitting the muzzle and handing the end of the leash to his visibly nervous wife. She squeezed past Lucas and disappeared with the dog.

All signs of belligerence in the man were gone. He obediently unlocked the security-door, stepped aside to allow Fleur in and led the way into the living-room.

It was a shabby room, comfortably, but not lavishly furnished and showing the usual signs of family life. On every flat surface there were framed photographs.

Wordlessly gesturing towards the couch, the man invited Fleur and Lucas to sit. Avoiding eye contact, he took the armchair opposite them.

She couldn't believe the change in his demeanour. All signs of threat had disappeared. It was almost as if he was relieved. No-one spoke. His wife brought in a tea-tray and silently began pouring tea.

Lucas waved away the proffered cup, but Fleur felt sorry for the woman and accepted, smiling her thanks. In the awkward silence, she carefully sipped the milky tea.

Not knowing where to look, she allowed her gaze to wander over the photos nearest her. They were of the teenage daughter of the house in various stages of growing up. There were photos of a boy, too. Hanging on a wall opposite Fleur could see an arrangement of Asian artefacts and military photos.

At last Lucas spoke, his voice still harsh. 'What is your real name?'

'Frank Viney.'

'Rank?'

'Private.'

It took a minute for Fleur to

understand his reason for the line of questioning. She realised Lucas had rightly summed up this man was ex-Army and that he would obey orders if they were issued firmly enough. It explained why he had capitulated. But it didn't explain why he had thought he could get away with impersonating Tom in the first place.

Impatient, Fleur leaned forward. 'You know Tom, don't you?'

At last he looked into her eyes. 'Yes,' he admitted.

'Where — '

'I think you had better tell us all about it,' interrupted Lucas, restraining her with a gentle hand on her arm.

'I saw your advertisement in the paper.' He turned to take a quick look at his wife behind him. 'Things haven't been very good since I got out of the Army. People . . . the government . . . ' For a moment, anger surfaced again. 'It wasn't my fault it was an unpopular war. I went where I was sent.'

Seemingly unmoved, Lucas kept up

the pressure. 'And you've been taking it out on everyone ever since,' he said in the same harsh voice, glancing meaningfully at the man's silent wife.

Frank Viney stiffened at the criticism. 'You people don't know what it was like coming home from that hell-hole to . . . '

There was a softer tone to Lucas' voice when he answered. 'No, we don't. But go on.'

'There's nothing more to say. I saw the advertisement and thought there could be some money in it.'

At last Lucas asked the question Fleur wanted to hear. 'Do you know what happened to Tom Drysdale?'

She held her breath, waiting.

The man couldn't disguise his scorn. 'Of course I do. I wouldn't have tried this on if I hadn't, would I? I'm not that silly.'

'Is he dead?' Fleur could hardly say the words.

Frank Viney turned his attention back to her. 'Dead? Where'd you get that idea?'

She took that to mean Tom was still alive, but it didn't offer much more. Where was he? Was he all right? Getting information from this man was like pulling teeth, slow and painful. Despairing, she turned with a silent appeal to Lucas.

He stood up. 'Come on, Fleur. This is obviously a matter for the police, the Fraud Squad.'

The returning belligerence in Frank Viney's attitude disappeared immediately. He stood up and faced Lucas. 'Sit down,' he begged in a conciliatory manner.

Lucas remained resolute. 'We've heard nothing but whingeing about how life has treated you. I suggest you take that fight to the Government through your Association.' He leaned into Viney's face. 'We want to know what happened to Tom Drysdale, nothing more, and we want to know it now. Or else.'

His last words were threat enough to reimpose his authority. The man turned and gave his wife a desperate look. To Fleur's surprise, the woman came and, without a trace of her earlier timidity, positioned herself between the two men.

'If you'll just sit down, Mr . . . er, Frank will tell you all about Tom.'

Fleur wondered how many times this woman had had to intervene between her tortured husband and the world. It must have been almost fifteen years since the last of the Australian troops came home from Vietnam.

Lucas appeared to allow himself to be persuaded and sat down beside her again. This was the first time she'd seen him working, and she had to admire his strategy.

'Frank,' prompted Mrs Viney.

'Tom and I were in the same platoon. We were mates. We . . . saw action together at Long Tan and were lucky to get out alive. We kept in touch when we got back here, but Tom couldn't settle. He didn't have a wife to come home to like me, not even a girlfriend.'

Regret and guilt at what her mother had done tugged at Fleur and must have shown on her face. Lucas' hand, that had somehow taken charge of hers, tightened sympathetically.

'He couldn't front up and go back into the schoolroom, didn't want an office job either, so he just took up labouring and the like. One day he announced he was going back to Vietnam.' Frank Viney's voice broke. 'Without me.'

The loss of his friend's companionship in the unfriendly environment of the times obviously affected him badly. He bent his head to hide his emotion. His wife touched his shaking shoulder lightly and carried on with the story.

'Tom often talked to me about the . . . effect of the war on the Vietnamese, especially the children. It haunted him . . . It haunted them all,' she said, as if that explained her husband's behaviour.

Fleur wondered if Tom was one of the veterans who didn't want to be found. Has he cut himself off from even his army mate? That possibility, when she and Lucas were so close to finding him, knotted her stomach.

'Do you know where Tom went in Vietnam?' probed Lucas.

Mrs Viney looked nervously at her husband and then back to Lucas.

'That's why we wanted the money,' she stammered. 'For Frank to go back there, too. On a visit.'

Lucas was unbending, his voice harsh. 'I asked do you know where he is?'

'Yes, we hear from him now and again. He has set up an orphanage for the street kids of Saigon.'

★ ★ ★

The aircraft dropped low over the flat fields and prepared to land at Ho Chi Minh City Airport. Suddenly the ground was close and rushing past at such a speed that the patchwork of the fields were one long blur to Fleur.

There had been no question that she

would make this journey; it just became a matter of how soon. But it was a long way from Australia and she'd hardly slept. During the enforced wait in Singapore she'd paced the terminal, unable to take an interest in the duty-free shopping, afraid of missing the connecting flight to Vietnam.

Although Lucas had assured her that all details had been attended to, bookings made, visas obtained, she questioned him for the first time. After all, they were going to a foreign country, one that had only just emerged from years of war.

The heat and humidity was like a wet blanket. How had anyone fought a war in these conditions? The buildings around the perimeter of the runway still showed signs of that war, wrecks cluttered the nearby fields, and stripped and abandoned vehicles lay rusting by the roadside.

The area around the hotel wasn't much better, but it was the only accommodation considered by the

Government to be suitable for foreign visitors. Fleur sank on to a couch, their luggage at her feet, whilst Lucas took both passports to the check-in desk.

At last Lucas returned. 'There's a problem,' he said. 'For tonight there's only a double room. Would that be all right with you?'

Overwhelmed by the journey and the strangeness of Asia, she was ready to agree to anything. 'Why not? If they're going to charge me more for occupying a double room, I don't mind. I've brought plenty of travellers' cheques.'

He looked at her, and hesitated, as if about to say something more, before bending to pick up their cabin luggage. 'I'll take my things to your room for the time being.'

'Sure,' she replied, too tired to question his actions, and, dragging one foot after the other, blindly followed the slight figure of the bell-boy.

She staggered into the allotted room, dropped her coat on a chair and fell across the bed. She felt Lucas struggle to turn back the covers under her, then remove her shoes before heaving the dead weight of her legs to lie them straight between the crisp sheets.

There was little she could do to make it easier for him. Waves of exhaustion clouded her consciousness so that she was only dimly aware of a warm, wet flannel outlining her face and a soft towel drying it. Each limp hand was lifted in turn, the fingers carefully separated, washed and dried before being put down.

Lucas' gentle touch soothed away the last of the tiring journey. She stirred to thank him but the efforts robbed her of the last of her energy. 'That feels . . . good,' she mumbled, letting her head flop back on to the pillow.

'Tell me about it tomorrow,' he murmured, laying a folded cold cloth across her forehead.

'Yes, tomorrow . . . Tom . . . '

Fleur opened her eyes to a strange room suffused by morning light. Momentarily confused, she pushed away the sheet that covered her and sat up abruptly. Where was she? How did she get there?

It didn't take long for her clouded mind to clear. She was in Vietnam. But why was she still in her travelling clothes? And what was Lucas doing sleeping in the armchair beside her bed? Still fully dressed, too. Was he on guard? Had there been a danger of some kind?

The movement woke him.

'What are you doing here?' she asked, unable to remember much of the night before.

He straightened in the chair and rubbed a hand over the roughness of his stubble. It went from there to rumple his hair.

'There was a mix-up in the booking. They only had one double room. You were so tired you don't remember.' He got up, stretched and began rummaging in his bag until he found light-weight trousers and a clean shirt. 'Things will be different tonight, two single rooms as per the booking.'

'And you slept all night in that chair?'

'I can sleep anywhere, it's part of the job, you know that.'

Oh, yes, the private investigator. Fleur realised she'd forgotten this trip was just a job for Lucas. They'd spent so much time together in the search for Tom that he had become part of her life. And, she thought a little sadly, after today, his job done, he would disappear from it.

Not even Camille would see him again. She sighed for her friend's impossible dream.

'Now, would you like me to order you some tea before I use the bathroom?' he asked, lifting the phone.

* * *

Bathed and breakfasted, they stepped out of the hotel. Fleur had never seen so many people. They were everywhere, overflowing from the pavement on to the wide road and mingling dangerously with the chaotic traffic, if one could use the word traffic.

It was so unlike Australia where the orderly lines of motor vehicles were controlled by regular sets of lights. Here, there was only an odd old truck belching smoke, and one or two battered Jeeps doing battle with what seemed to her to be thousands of bicycles.

And hundreds of small motorbikes.

Noisily weaving in and out, some of them carried impossible loads of goods, others had several tiny figures clinging, without sign of fear, on their back.

Horns beeped, brakes squealed and dust and the stench of petrol fumes filled the air.

With an arm protectively at her back he directed her toward the line of bicycle-taxis parked in the hotel forecourt.

The cyclo was surprisingly comfortable and Fleur wished she could sit back and enjoy the novel experience like a tourist. She couldn't. Her whole being was concentrated on the reason for being in this country and nothing could divert her thoughts from that for long.

Her nerves strung tight with anticipation, she leaned forward on the edge of the seat as they left the main thoroughfare.

The street narrowed into alleyways with unmade surfaces that rocked the cyclo from side to side with every pothole. Fearful of being thrown out, Fleur clutched at Lucas' arm.

The rough section didn't last long. They eventually emerged into a tiny square. The sinewy legs of the taxi-man stopped pedalling beside a high stone wall.

Even to Fleur's impatient mind, the ride to the orphanage had gone quickly. She got down and looked about her at what she guessed must have been Tom's neighbourhood for years.

A relic of the French colonisation of Vietnam, but obviously neglected during the long war, the buildings were old and run down.

A group of westerners on tour was disembarking from a mini-bus at the entrance. Lucas and Fleur joined them as their Vietnamese guide led the way to the heavy wooden door. The sound of children at play reached them.

A pulse throbbed in Fleur's forehead and she could feel her heart beating strongly against her rib-cage. This was it, the moment of truth. Her search was over, she was going to see Tom! Would she still know him? Would he know her?

The children's shouts grew louder as the group moved through the gate and fanned out into a large courtyard.

Fleur's first reaction was to laugh. A game of cricket was in progress. How very Australian! But there was nothing Australian about the slight figures spread out as fieldsmen, their attention concentrated on the Asian child with a cricket bat almost as big as himself.

Her eyes went past the children to the tall figure directing play from behind the stumps.

13

The years had not changed Tom's appearance. He still stood straight, and the sun-tanned face under the old slouch hat was as Fleur remembered it, a little older looking, but still her Tom.

Childish voices began singing in a class-room at the other end of the courtyard. It was as if the intervening years had never been, and the two of them were back in a Melbourne suburban schoolyard, young and in love, their life stretching ahead of them. Until the war came.

There was a flurry at the crease and the batsman was out. His was obviously the last wicket to fall. The game ended and the young players happily clustered around Tom.

Fleur stood still, torn between the past and the reality of the here and now, and uncertain of her next move.

She realised that in the weeks of searching she hadn't once thought beyond finding Tom.

A Vietnamese woman came out of a covered way behind the group and introduced herself to the visitors.

'If you'll come this way, I'll show you through the orphanage,' she said in softly-accented English. 'As you can see, the building is old and needs repair, but we do our best with our limited resources, for which we depend entirely on overseas donations.'

Fleur let go of Lucas' hand and allowed herself to be drawn into the group tour of inspection, hardly aware of what the woman was saying, a large part of her mind wrestling with her mixed feelings.

She was glad to have come to the end of her search, to have found Tom at last. She wasn't sure of what she'd expected, but it certainly wasn't this sense of anti-climax. And strangely, the need to tell him exactly what had happened to his letters no longer seemed urgent.

Was it because he looked so well and more importantly, so happy? She asked herself had she expected him to be still carrying a torch for her? He obviously had been able to get on with his life.

She had to admit she hadn't. At least, not until his letters had been found. Her heart had been closed to all but memories, afraid to perhaps find another love and again be rejected. It had been safer to build her life around school and her mother.

Which was what Elaine Mitchell had intended when she intercepted Tom's letters.

In a daze, Fleur looked back over her shoulder, but he had gone, taking the children with him. The courtyard was empty.

★　★　★

The conducted tour of the orphanage reached the dormitories. They were all spotlessly clean but, to her western eyes, the big rooms of closely-packed camping-cots seemed pitifully inadequate. She was glad when they moved on for a quick look into the empty classrooms.

'The children would now like to perform for you,' announced the guide, opening fold-away doors to an assembly room. A sea of smiling faces gave the guests a traditional greeting, encouraged by Tom.

She watched him from the back of the room as the young orphans displayed their musical skills. Phillip Bennett had been right. Tom had fulfilled the headmaster's prediction for him and become a good teacher, one who was obviously proud of his pupils.

But more than that, he'd survived what had been a horrible war that left many scarred for life, and he'd gone back to help the war-ravaged country. That fitted in with what she remembered of him and his beliefs of brotherly love.

Still unsure of what she should do, Fleur looked for their guide. She wished she'd caught the name when the woman introduced herself. There was something beautifully calm about the face, almost familiar.

Fleur wondered if perhaps it was because, in the brief time she and Lucas had been in the country, she'd become accustomed to seeing only gentle Vietnamese faces.

Fleur didn't have time to wonder. The children's songs had ended and with an excited rush they exited to the courtyard. Tom smiled after them before giving his full attention to the group of visitors.

The smile still on his face, he put out his hand and began to greet each one in turn.

'Thank you for coming.'

Fleur knew what was about to happen. She stood and waited for him, as she had for almost twenty years.

At last, Tom's hand was in hers, firm and impersonal.

'Thank — ' he began.

When she first entered the courtyard

and saw him she'd been engulfed by memories. Now it was his turn.

She saw recognition flash into his eyes, remembrance register on his face and stifle his words.

'Your letters were lost and only just found,' she explained in a low voice for him alone.

His grip on her hand tightened as he comprehended her message.

The familiar voice deepened and used the same words to her as he had to the others, but this time they were rich with meaning.

'Thank you for coming,' he said, before letting go and moving on to the next tourist.

The last thank you said, and the visit over, the group broke up. As they walked toward the gate someone in the crowd exclaimed, 'Aren't they a wonderful couple!'

A couple? Fleur looked back. Tom was standing beside the woman, an arm across her shoulders, holding her close to his body. It was plain that after the horror that was the Vietnam war, he had found happiness with this woman.

Fleur realised she was genuinely glad for him.

★ ★ ★

There wasn't much said on the way back to the hotel. As if respecting her privacy, Lucas didn't press her to talk about what had happened between her and Tom.

If he thought it odd that she could walk away after her efforts to find Tom, he didn't comment. He had become the private investigator again, treating her with consideration. As you would a client, she reminded herself. Not a friend.

Their conversation, as they prepared for the long journey home, was of practical matters. During the waiting time in Singapore airport he encouraged Fleur to do some shopping, bargaining for her whilst she bought a silk blouse for her mother and perfume for Camille.

In the long silences of the flight, Fleur's mind had been on Tom. She thought of the good he was doing for a second generation, the children of the innocent victims of a war that had orphaned their mothers and left them on the streets. She wondered what she could do to help him in his work.

It was only as they approached Melbourne airport and the demands of her daily life encroached on her thinking that she remembered that that life would not include Lucas.

'Home safely, mission accomplished,' he said as the aircraft landed with a slight bump and the roar of reversing engines.

Fleur stared back at the now familiar face with the piercing blue eyes. The private investigator eyes. A lump rose in her throat. She already missed him.

★ ★ ★

Nothing was said during the walk down endless corridors to immigration and the retrieval of their luggage from the grinding carousel. When they came out of the terminal, not even the shock of a Melbourne winter after the steaminess of Asia could loosen her tongue. There didn't seem to be anything to say.

Except goodbye.

That was quite formal when the time came. Lucas lifted her case from the car and stood with it while her cold fingers fitted the key in the front door, but she hardly noticed.

Fleur turned back to him with a thank-you.

'I'm glad I've been able to help you, Fleur. It's been a pleasure,' he said, shaking her hand before leaving her and striding down the path to his car. Without looking back.

She wanted to think there'd been a flash of something special in his eyes as he'd left, but she couldn't be sure. Her own were brimming.

And if he'd waved a last goodbye

from his car she would never know, the tears had become a blinding curtain.

★　★　★

'I didn't expect you back so soon. I told you it was a wild-goose chase,' Elaine Mitchell greeted her daughter. 'And a waste of money,' she added.

'It wasn't a wild-goose chase, Mother. We found Tom.'

Her mother gave a little start.

'Well, where is he?'

'Still in Vietnam, running an orphan-age.'

'You went all that way and didn't bring him back with you?'

Something akin to relief crossed her face, followed immediately by another more troubled look. 'You aren't think-ing of going there to live with him, are you?'

Fleur smiled. Her mother was so transparent.

'No, Mother, I'm not going to live in Vietnam.'

'Did you tell him what happened? What did you say?'

'I told him his letters had been lost and only just found.'

Elaine Mitchell was incredulous. 'Was that all you said?' she asked, as if she wanted to be sure there was no chance she'd have to face Tom and admit to her wrong-doing.

Fleur smiled. She knew it would be difficult for her mother to understand, making it hardly worth her trying to explain.

'There was no need to tell him what had actually happened to the letters. We always understood each other,' she replied in a firm voice intended to let her mother know it was the end of the discussion. That chapter of her life was over.

Her mother looked hard at her. She wasn't used to her daughter using that tone of voice to her.

'But there is something I want to talk to you about,' Fleur went on. 'The orphanage desperately needs money. I thought you could start an auxiliary in the retirement village. There must be lots of women here who are still not arthritic and are good with their hands. Why don't you get them making saleable items like knitted scarves and caps? Even baby layettes. Or strike cuttings for the garden.

'Camille and I will take a stall at the weekend market to sell them. It would be a good thing for war widows to help victims of war, don't you think?'

Her mother gave her another hard look. Fleur couldn't bring herself to add that in some ways it might make up for the wrong that had been done.

More cheerful now that the danger of confrontation with Tom had passed, Elaine Mitchell began making plans to organise the women as if it was all her own idea.

★   ★   ★

The narrow alley-way where Lucas had his office looked even more discouraging at night, the old-style lamps throwing isolated pools of light that left the rest of the street in shadows.

Fleur hesitated, glancing back at her parked car. She was taking a risk, she knew that, and it wasn't only with her safety.

The building was in darkness except for a faint light showing in an upper storey window. She reached out a shaking hand to press the security button.

'Yes?'

'Lucas, it's Fleur.'

There was a moment of silence. A last-minute doubt niggled. Was this such a good idea after all? When she realised she'd let him into her heart, she'd agonised over what action to take.

The first thing she'd done was confess her feelings to Camille. Her friend had been nonchalant about the news.

'I'm not surprised, really, just surprised it took you so long to wake up to

149

it. He always showed more than a businesslike interest in you.'

Fleur quietened the surge of optimism. 'You're not upset?' she asked.

'No, of course not,' Camille assured her. 'You know my motto. Never run after a bus, there'll be another one along soon.'

Fleur had laughed and hugged her friend.

But one question remained and only she could answer it. Should she give up waiting and go to Lucas? So much of her life had been spent doing nothing, and denying herself any chance at happiness. Reluctant to waste any more time, she had decided to take the risk.

'Fleur!' Lucas' voice over the intercom was a mixture of surprise and pleasure.

The door buzzed. As she pushed it open the stairwell lights went on. She began climbing. Above her, she could hear the thud of footsteps descending the stairs two at a time. Lucas was not waiting for her, he was coming to meet her. In a hurry. The last of her doubts disappeared.

They met on the landing outside his closed office.

Suddenly shy, Fleur felt she needed to make an excuse for being there. 'I was passing and saw your light.'

'Passing?'

The ridiculousness of it had them both laughing.

'Come on up,' he urged, leading the way up a further flight of stairs and into a comfortably-furnished room, lit only by a standard lamp beside one end of the couch. Mozart was being played softly on the stereo.

'So this is where you live,' Fleur remarked, looking around.

He swept the business papers on the coffee table into a tidy pile and invited her to join him on the couch. They both spoke at once.

'Not on surveillance — ?'

'I began to think you weren't — '

Lucas gave a short laugh. 'After you.'

Fleur shook her head. 'No, no, it was

nothing. What were you saying?'

'I began to think you weren't coming.'

'Sorry? Did we have an appointment?'

'In a way, yes. I was hoping that, given time, you would come.'

Fleur knew what hoping was all about. And waiting. She had waited hopefully to hear from Tom after he went to war. There had eventually been a happy ending to that long wait when she and Lucas had found him in Vietnam. Lucas hadn't known it but that day had freed her from the past. And from the helplessness of waiting.

'Hoping?' she teased, wanting to hear more. 'Do I owe you money? You could've had your office girl call me.'

His piercing blue, private investigator's eyes held hers. 'You know what I mean. I wasn't sure your search for Tom was really over.'

The time for playing games had ended. 'Going to Vietnam was about righting a wrong, not looking for love. I had already found it by then.' But didn't know it, she might have added.

There was nothing of the private investigator in his gaze, only a man's longing, held in check.

'Whatever happened to the shy schoolteacher who came to me for help?' he asked with mock surprise, but reassuringly, his hands had found hers.

Fleur asked herself the same question but couldn't allow answering it in detail to deflect her honesty. 'I fell in love,' she said bravely.

The grip on her hands tightened, almost painfully. 'You know that with my job, I don't have the right to ask anyone to share my life. It would be too hard, too lonely for them.'

'You use the word share. Doesn't sharing your life mean just that? A partnership?'

The beginnings of a smile was creeping over Lucas' face. 'Are you suggesting . . . ?'

'You're a smart man, don't tell me you hadn't thought of that. Two heads are better than one, they say. Wouldn't that apply particularly to the investigating business? You have to admit we work well together.'

'Yes, yes, we do, but . . . my marriage was a disaster. Didn't last any time at all. It couldn't handle the demands made on it, with me keeping the hours . . . '

'It's different now. You were very young then, just getting started. And anyway, that was in the past. Like Tom.' She leaned closer. 'The past,' she repeated softly.

'Your argument is most compelling, Miss Mitchell.' He tried to make a joke of it, but his voice was tight with constraint. 'I am almost tempted . . . to believe it.'

'Would this help with your decision-making?' Surprised at herself, Fleur boldly reached out a hand to caress the back of his head. Gently, she increased the pressure but Lucas resisted. He clearly had more to say.

'I was attracted to you the first day

you walked in, but I learned you were looking for a lost love,' he said.

Fleur was certain she could feel a slight relaxation of his stiff body. She took a deep breath, determined to press home her advantage, but before she could speak, he went on.

'A lost love, not a new love,' he reminded her. 'And once I was employed by you, my business ethics prevented me making any claims on your feelings.'

'But you did make a claim on my feelings,' she said triumphantly. 'By being yourself.' She leaned farther forward and gave the tantalising mouth so close to hers a brief but warm kiss. 'I rest my case.'

At the touch of her lips, Lucas' resistance crumpled. His arms went out to wrap themselves around her body, then tightened and pulled her up close. All in one swift movement.

'Fleur, Fleur,' he groaned into her hair. 'You were such a worry to me, taking risks . . . '

For several wondrous moments, she nestled against the wildly-beating heart that matched the rhythm of her own. At last, he held her away from himself to examine her face closely.

'Are you sure about this?'

Sure? How could he even ask? Fleur knew she couldn't be more sure of anything; being in his arms felt so right. Her search for love over, there was only one answer to that.

'I'm sure,' she said, and smiled.

In the time she'd known him, she'd never before seen the look that came over Lucas' face, a look of unbelievable happiness. She guessed it probably mirrored her own, if she was to go by how she felt.

Other titles in the
Linford Romance Library:

HER HEART'S DESIRE

Dorothy Taylor

When Beth Garland's great aunt Emily dies, she leaves Greg, her boyfriend, in Manchester — along with her successful advertising job — to return to live in Emily's cottage. Feeling disillusioned with Greg and his high-handed attitude, she finds herself more and more attracted to her aunt's gardener, Noah. But Noah seems to be hiding from the past, whilst Greg has his own ideas about the direction of their relationship. Surrounded by secrecy and deceit, how will Beth ever find true love?

PRECIOUS MOMENTS

June Gadsby

The heartbreak was all behind her, but hearing her name mentioned on the radio, and that song — their special song — brought bittersweet memories rushing back through the years. It had to be a coincidence, and was best forgotten — but then Lara opened the door to find her past standing there. The moment of truth she had dreaded for years had finally arrived, and she wasn't sure how to handle it . . .

THE SECRET OF SHEARWATER

Diney Delancey

When Zoe Carson inherits a cottage in Cornwall, she takes a holiday from her job in London to stay at the cottage. There, she makes friends with the local people, including the hot-tempered Gregory Enodoc. Zoe is glad of their friendship when events take a sinister turn and the police become involved. And when she decides to leave London to live permanently at the cottage, Zoe is unaware of the dangers into which this will lead her . . .